TOEFL
托福文法與構句

李英松／著

下冊

n't have a carefully developed plot. (主格補語) Whatever you decide will be fin
at red bicycle. (介詞的受詞) Do you know what ha ed
The p r gave whatever spots to the rest of my tun ndwic
had nother coat of enamel. (間接受詞) Roth mowed the our
e ho d out the weeds, while we weeded ds.
d no he roses. Give some consideration e se eve y
, ours in the hot sun had 形容詞子句──當做形容詞
us feel as though the day would never end.
ist of of people and some that contain is a group
ang e language that we use during our childhoo
tio y 立子句（或稱主要子句），可以單獨存在成為
e. 可以和另外一個獨立子句連結，The gymnasts and the
d me 能完整表達意思。William read The Washington Post
station. (句) Our class is writing stories for the second graders at Thomson Elementary Sch
to subway station, and I arrived at school on time. (兩個

自序

　　愚公移山的寓言故事，以及「滴水能穿石,鐵杵能磨針」的古人名言，再再的告訴我們要完成偉大的事業或者是鉅大的工程，一定要有堅持到底的決心與恆心。古人又提醒我們「工欲善其事，必先利其器　」，用現代的白話文來說，意思就是，我們要做好任何事；一定要將工具準備好，並且要用對方法。

　　我們從小到大，已經參加無數的考試，考試所需要的工具，除了上課的教科書之外，其它的參考書籍也是不可缺少。

　　在這個熙攘繁忙的現代社會，我們每天都面臨了各式各樣的壓力，擁擠的交通，忙碌的家事和競爭的職場與試場，讓我們從早到晚活在喘不過氣當中。

　　我們要拋開過去失敗的痛苦，停止為將來的事情擔憂，活在當下，相信現在是我們唯一能掌控的。過去的事情已經無法改變，未來則取決於我們現在的作為。

　　本系列書「托福文法與構句」前冊、上冊、中冊和下冊共四冊書到此全部出版。再加上本系列書的姊妹作「托福字彙」上冊、中冊、下冊一和下冊二共八冊書，都是筆者針對托福考試的內容，收集資料編著成書，以供讀者應付托福考試參考之用。

　　筆者無法免俗，只好老王賣瓜，自賣自誇，有志參加托福考試的讀者們，如果能夠研讀這八冊書，並且不斷的自我測檢，獲得托福考試的高分，必是指日可待。筆者此時此刻，預祝各位順順利利的通過托福考試，高高興興的踏上留學的旅途。

目錄

第廿章 | 托福文法總複習題目與解答

1.　She couldn't consult the map because it was (packing/packed) away.

　　＜解答＞ packed

2.　The people (was/were) given small party favors.

　　＜解答＞ were

3.　(The New York City/New York City) is the largest city in New York.

　　＜解答＞ New York City

4.　The newspaper is on (table/the table).

　　＜解答＞ the table

5.　(A/The) sugar spilled on the floor.

　　＜解答＞ The

6.　Tennis is (more/as) boring than football.

　　＜解答＞ more

7.　Golf is the (most/more) boring game.

　　＜解答＞ most

8.　Jack is as happy (as/than) a clown.

　　＜解答＞ as

9.　Jack is (less/least) happy than he was last year.

　　＜解答＞ less

10.　He is the (happier/happiest) person I know.

　　＜解答＞ happiest

11.　Lee eats the (least/less) slowly of all his friends.

　　＜解答＞ least

12. My boat sails (fast/faster) than yours.

    ＜解答＞ faster

13. She sails the (fastest/fast).

    ＜解答＞ fastest

14. The deck is (more longer/longer) than the counch.

    ＜解答＞ longer

15. Today's lecture was (most/more) stimulating than ever before.

    ＜解答＞ more

16. If I (know/knew) his number, I'd call him now.

    ＜解答＞ knew

17. If she (had helped/helped), we would have finished.

    ＜解答＞ had helped

18. (We had/Had we) known, we would have brought a gift.

    ＜解答＞ Had we

19. We would have enjoyed ourselves more (if you/you) had been there.

    ＜解答＞ if you

20. I would answer truthfully if I (was/were) you.

    ＜解答＞ were

21. If he (was/were) younger, he would join.

    ＜解答＞ were

22. The suggestion was to skim and then (scanning/to scan) for information.

    ＜解答＞ to scan

23. It didn't matter whether the report was typed (and/or) handwritten.

    ＜解答＞ or

24. The books were left (in/on) the table.

    ＜解答＞ on

25. I run into him (on/from) time to time.

    ＜解答＞ from

26. The audience came (from out of/out of) the auditorium.

    ＜解答＞ out of

27. Since it was their vacation, it should be their decision how to spend (them/it).
    ＜解答＞ it

28. Compared to you and (I/me), Maureen is extremely studious.
    ＜解答＞ me

29. The problem was a complex one, so we needed ample time (to discuss/to discuss it).
    ＜解答＞ to discuss it

30. John and his roommate (they have to/have to) get up early to get to class on time.
    ＜解答＞ have to

31. (Children and youngsters/Children) should enjoy the holidays.
    ＜解答＞ Children

32. The book is (free gratis/free).
    ＜解答＞ free

33. He did it (perfectly/perfectly without a mistake).
    ＜解答＞ perfectly

34. The squirel (put the food/stored the food and put it) away.
    ＜解答＞ put the food

35. I'll meet him when (comes/he comes).
    ＜解答＞ he comes

36. Telling their professor the truth (this made/made) them feel better.
    ＜解答＞ made

37. It was necessary that he (knew/know) the formula.
    ＜解答＞ know

38. It will be recommended that she (will get/get) the job.
    ＜解答＞ get

39. He asked his tutor what (A. is the right way to solve a problem/B. The right way to solve a problem is).
    ＜解答＞ B

40. Classes were cancelled (because there/there) was so much snow.
    ＜解答＞　because there

41. Although (some passers-by witnessed/witnessed) the theft, no one would
    testify.
    ＜解答＞　some passers-by witnessed

42. The orchestra (which it/which) had cancelled all performances has disbanded.
    ＜解答＞　which

43. We will be ready to start (while/when) he comes.
    ＜解答＞　when

44. The winner, (was ecstatic/ecstatic) about the results, jumped up and down.
    ＜解答＞　ecstatic

45. He asked what time (was it/it was).
    ＜解答＞　it was

46. (The research/That the research) had been easy astounded him.
    ＜解答＞　That the research

47. Whose essays were missing (were/was) on everyone's mind.
    ＜解答＞　was

48. His name, which (I had/had) known before, escaped me.
    ＜解答＞　I had

49. They took the steps because of the elevator, (which was/which) broken.
    ＜解答＞　which was

50. We beckoned to the waitress (who she/who) was so busy.
    ＜解答＞　who

51. The book (was/which was) required reading was being held at the reference
    desk.
    ＜解答＞　which was

52. The campus, which had become desolate and deserted (A. during the holidays,
    suddenly came to life again/B. during the holidays).
    ＜解答＞　A

53. The girls (who/which) won were honored by their friends.

    ＜解答＞ who

54. Although (witnessed/some witnessed) the theft, no one would testify.

    ＜解答＞ some witnessed

55. They took a small gift in case (she/she was) depressed.

    ＜解答＞ she was

56. Classess were cancelled because there was (so/very) much snow.

    ＜解答＞ so

57. After driving for days across the desert without seeing (A. another living thing, we ran out of gas/B. another living thing).

    ＜解答＞ A

58. (He having/Having) quit school, the student found a job.

    ＜解答＞ Having

59. The winner, ecstatic about the result, (jumped up/up) and down.

    ＜解答＞ jumped up

60. He was proud to see his grades (which posted/posted) on the bulletin board.

    ＜解答＞ posted

61. The teacher, (reviewing/reviewed) for the test, asked if there were questions.

    ＜解答＞ reviewing

62. While (she singing/singing) the anthem, she had tears in her eyes.

    ＜解答＞ singing

63. Daniel waited, (was getting/getting) more and more nervous until the moment arrived.

    ＜解答＞ getting

64. (The alarm going off/Hearing the alarm go off), victor got out of bed.

    ＜解答＞ Hearing the alarm go off

65. (While reading/Reading), she keeps her headphones on.

    ＜解答＞ While reading

66. After (talked/talking) to the counselor, the student enrolled in the course.

    ＜解答＞ talking

67. The students (will have/will) completed the essay by the end of the class.
    ＜解答＞ will have

68. The messenger (did delivered/delivered) the package.
    ＜解答＞ delivered

69. The news of their successes (were/was) met with cheers.
    ＜解答＞ was

70. I'm going to eat as soon as the cafeteria (opens/will open).
    ＜解答＞ opens

71. The ocean was two miles (depth/deep) at that point.
    ＜解答＞ deep

72. The fruit tasted (bitter/bitterly).
    ＜解答＞ bitter

73. They wondered (where was he/where he was).
    ＜解答＞ where he was

74. There (the door is/is the door).
    ＜解答＞ is the door

75. Around the table (sat the directors/the directors sat).
    ＜解答＞ sat the directors

76. Only if he comes, (I will come/will I come), too.
    ＜解答＞ will I come

77. (He had come/Had he come), we would have finished.
    ＜解答＞ Had he come

78. (Never he has/Never has he) done that.
    ＜解答＞ Never has he

79. (Intelligent anyone/Anyone intelligent) could do it.
    ＜解答＞ Anyone intelligent

80. (The girl in the shout dress/In the short dress, the girl) looked ridiculous.
    ＜解答＞ The girl in the shout dress

81. The event was (well-planned extremely/extremely well-planned).
    ＜解答＞ extremely well-planned

82. He used a (A. Japanese, new, lightweight, black, compact/B. compact, lightweight, new, black, Japanese) camera.
    ＜解答＞ B

83. If one lives in Florida one day and in Iceland the next, he is (certainly/certain) to feel the change in temperature.
    ＜解答＞ certain

84. The industrial trend is in the direction of more machines and (fewer/less) people.
    ＜解答＞ fewer

85. At last, late in the afternoon, a long line of flags and colored umbrellas (were/was) seen moving toward the gate of the palace.
    ＜解答＞ was

86. Psychologists and psychiatrists will tell us that it is of utmost importance that a disturbed child (receives/receive) professional attention as soon as possible.
    ＜解答＞ receive

87. That angry outburst of Father's last night was so annoying that it resulted in our (guests/guests') packing up and leaving this morning.
    ＜解答＞ guests'

88. An acquaintance with the memoirs of Elizabeth Barrett Browning and Robert Browning (enables/enable) us to appreciate the depth of influence that two people of talent can have on each other.
    ＜解答＞ enables

89. If he (would have/had) lain quietly as instructed by the doctor, he might not have had a second heart attack.
    ＜解答＞ had

90. Mrs. Adams was (surprise/surprised) that her son and his friend had gone to the mountains to ski.
    ＜解答＞ surprised

91. Although Elmer did not look line his brother, (there/their) personalities were very similar.

<解答> their

92. Between one thing and another, Julie (did not/does not) finish her work in time to go to the show last night.

    <解答> did not

93. If Paul had wanted to pass his exams, he (would have studied/would have study) much harder for them.

    <解答> would have studied

94. Except for (you and I/you and me), everyone is enjoying this new play, it seems.

    <解答> you and me

95. Having attended college (since/for) four years, Nana is quite proficient at taking notes.

    <解答> for

96. (As/Like) his sister, David needed a ride from some generous person in order to get home.

    <解答> Like

97. Each man and woman must sign (his or her/their) full name before entering the examination room.

    <解答> his or her

98. From the top of the tower, Mitch was able to see the whole city (clear and easy/clearly and easily) stretched out below him.

    <解答> clearly and easily

99. I have studied very hard for my finals this term because unless I pass all of them, (its/it's) the end of my scholarship.

    <解答> it's

100. The day before yesterday, June (had/had had) dessert at the ice cream parlor, but today she will buy pastries at the bakery instead.

    <解答> had

101. Jessica is only an amateur, but she sings (sweeter/more sweetly) than most professionals.

<解答＞　more sweetly

102. An old miser (who/which) picked up yellow pieces of gold had something of the simple order of a child who picks out yellow flowers.
<解答＞　who

103. Although Marilyn was not invited to the wedding, she would very much have liked (to go/to have gone).
<解答＞　to go

104. The inexperienced teacher had difficulty in controlling the students whom she was escorting on a visit to the chemical factory, because it (stank/stunk) so.
<解答＞　stank

105. Since I loved her very much when she was alive, I prize my (mother's-in-law/mother-in-law's) picture and I wouldn't sell it for all the money in the world.
<解答＞　mother-in-law's

106. Lie detectors measure physiological changes in respiration, perspiration, muscular grip, and (how the blood presure is/blood presure).
<解答＞　blood presure

107. After studying hard to become an accountant, he discovered that (it/accounting) was not what he wanted to do.
<解答＞　accounting

108. Joel rediculed (Anna/Anna's) taking vitamins because he believed that they were useless.
<解答＞　Anna's

109. Henry is the one correspondent who writes letters more quickly (than/that) I can answer them.
<解答＞　than

110. (Eating/Having eaten) the cherry pie, I struck several pits and nearly broke a tooth.
<解答＞　Eating

111. A boy (whom/who) you must meet right away is Freddy Thompson, the best math student in our dormitory.

    ＜解答＞ whom

112. I don't know (as/whether) you can recognize her from here, but the girel reading the newspaper is Susan.

    ＜解答＞ whether

113. Bobby's three favorite pastimes are playing chess, working out the gym, and (he likes to read/reading) mysteries.

    ＜解答＞ reading

114. I intended (to have written/to write) her a letter yesterday, but I forgot to because of the day and evening appointments that I had.

    ＜解答＞ to write

115. (Cliff/Cliff's) and Al's car broke down again, but luckily they knew how to fix it.

    ＜解答＞ Cliff

116. Of the three plants Amy had in her apartment, only the ivy, which is (the hardier/the hardiest), lived through the winter.

    ＜解答＞ the hardiest

117. Jerry will not lend you the book because he is fearful (that/if) you will forget to return it.

    ＜解答＞ that

118. When he retires, Professor Jones (will be/will have been) teaching here for over thirty years, but his classes are never dull.

    ＜解答＞ will have been

119. We were terrified by sounds: the (screamings/screaming's) of the wind; the restles rustle of leaves in the trees; and the sudden, overwhelming explosions of thunder.

    ＜解答＞ screamings

120. Your employer would have been inclined to favor your request if you (had/would have) waited for an occasion when he was less busy with other

more important matters.

　＜解答＞　had

121. After all the performers had finished their performances, I knew the winner to be (he/him) whom I had singled out the moment I had met him.

　＜解答＞　him

122. Struggling hard against almost insuperable adds, he was unable, to effect even a small change in the (course/coarse) of the vehicle.

　＜解答＞　course

123. Looking through the main gate at the southwest corner of the park where the bridle path emerges from the wood, (the blooming lilac can be seen/we can see the blooming lilac) in great sprays of purple, lavender, and white.

　＜解答＞　we can see the blooming lilac

124. (Irregardless/Regardless) of what you believe, I know that Sam never hurt anyone, least of all his best friend.

　＜解答＞　Regardless

125. Charlie assured his wife that there was no danger, but she could not help (worrying/but worry).

　＜解答＞　worrying

126. (We looked back/Looking back), the house seemed to have been engulfed by the snow, which fell faster and faster.

　＜解答＞　We looked back

127. Cathy arrived so late that she could not find anyone to carry the luggage (she brings/she brought).

　＜解答＞　she brought

128. I want everyone (to set/to sit) in his own seat before I serve dinner.

　＜解答＞　to sit

129. The astrophysicist claimed that in about a million years the earth (will melt/would melt).

　＜解答＞　would melt

130. I had hoped (to learn/to have learned) French before my trip to Paris, but I did not have any extra money for a course.

    ＜解答＞ to learn

131. Emily shops only in stores that have inexpensive goods, a friendly atmosphere, and (a convenient location/that are conveniently located).

    ＜解答＞ a convenient location

132. Although how a steam engine works is widely known, we still cannot (doubt that/doubt but that) some people have never heard of steam engines.

    ＜解答＞ doubt that

133. You should try Larry and Kevin's restaurant because (their's/theirs) is the best.

    ＜解答＞ theirs

134. (These/This) pair of shoes look too small, but I'd like to try them on.

    ＜解答＞ This

135. You must remit tuition whether you (were/was) here during the hurricane or not.

    ＜解答＞ were

136. Separate vacations by husband and wife are much esteemed in certain circles, but if such holidays last more than a year or so, even the most liberal raise (their/there) eyebrow.

    ＜解答＞ their

137. The captain of the squad was a sophomore, one of last (years/year's) freshman team, a player of great intelligence, and, above all, endurance.

    ＜解答＞ year's

138. No one who has seen him work in the laboratory can deny that William has an (interest in/interest) and an aptitude for chemical experimentation.

    ＜解答＞ interest in

139. The reason teenagers tend to follow the trend while openly declaring themselves nonconformists is (that/because) they are really insecure.

    ＜解答＞ that

140. A great many educations firmly believe that English is one of the (most poorly/poorest) taught subjects in high school today.

　　＜解答＞ most poorly

141. After I (had listened/listened) to the violonist and cellist, and enjoyed their interpretations, I hurried home to practice.

　　＜解答＞ had listened

142. (Having sat/Having set) the bag of dirty clothes on a bench in the apartment building laundry room, Mrs. Lee chatted with a neighbor until a washing machine was available.

　　＜解答＞ Having set

143. It was our neighbor's opinion that if Kennedy (was/were) alive today, the country would have fewer problems than it has now.

　　＜解答＞ were

144. If anyone in the audience has anything to add to what the speaker has already said, let (him/them) speak up.

　　＜解答＞ him

145. Neither rain nor snow nor sleet (keep/keeps) the postman from delivering our letters which we so much look forward to receiving.

　　＜解答＞ keeps

146. Bob could easily have gotten a higher score on his college entrance test if he (had read/would have read) more in his school career.

　　＜解答＞ had read

147. When my aunt and uncle's plane (arrives/arrive) at the airport in San Diego, I shall already have left San Diego for Mexico City.

　　＜解答＞ arrives

148. Cesar Chavez, president of the United Farm workers Union, called for a Congressional investigation of certain California lettuce growers (who/whom), he said, were giving bribes to a rival union.

　　＜解答＞ who

149. The girl who won the beauty contest in (nowhere near/not nearly) as beautiful as my mother was when she was a bried.

　　＜解答＞ not nearly

150. Even if Detroit could provide (nonpolluting/nonpolluted) cars by the original deadline to meet precribed Federal standards for clean air, the effect in big cities would be slight because only new cars would be properly equipped.

＜解答＞ nonpolluting

151. The sun (hadn't hardly/had hardly) set when the mosquitoes began to sting so annoyingly that we had to run off from the picnic grounds.

＜解答＞ had hardly

152. A wise and experienced administrator will assign a job to (whomever/whoever) is best qualified.

＜解答＞ whoever

153. Unless there can be some assurance of increased pay, factory morale, (already/all ready) low, will collapse completely.

＜解答＞ already

154. As she was small, her huge eyes and her long black hair were neither outstanding (or/nor) attractive.

＜解答＞ nor

155. If we are given the opportunity to stage a play, (whose/who's) to decide which play we shall produce ?

＜解答＞ who's

156. More leisure, as well as an abundance of goods, (is/are) attainable through automation.

＜解答＞ is

157. The founder and, for many years, the guiding spirit of the " Kenyon Review " is John Crowe Ransom, (whom/who) you must know as an outstanding American critic.

＜解答＞ whom

158. The children reported that the object of the game their teacher (had taught/had learned) them was to kick a ball across the field.

＜解答＞ had taught

159. Apparently (angered/angry) by several recent thefts, Mr. Jones hired two more watchmen.

　　＜解答＞ angered

160. The teacher anxiously told us that under such circumstances we must not regard (ourselves/ourself) the only ones that can succeed.

　　＜解答＞ ourselves

161. In one of his classes at school, Alan Masters had been studying about money and (its/his) importance in our business system.

　　＜解答＞ its

162. If we had no money, we would try to save goods until we (needed/need) them.

　　＜解答＞ needed

163. It was (considerable/considerate) of you not to play the piano while your mother had a bad headache.

　　＜解答＞ considerate

164. It is certainly true that we of this age should (lie/lay) emphasis upon the significantly educational goal we wish to attain.

　　＜解答＞ lay

165. When a store, a factory, or an office pays (its/their) workers for time spent at their jobs, business transactions are taking place.

　　＜解答＞ its

166. Habits formed while we are young become (fixed/firm fixed) as we grow older.

　　＜解答＞ fixed

167. The quicker a loan is repaid, the (least/less) it will cost.

　　＜解答＞ less

168. Do you think (its/it's) going to rain tomorrow ?

　　＜解答＞ it's

169. Gaining knowledge such as this (is/are) a good reason for travel, but a far better one is the broadening effect of contact with strangers in other lands.

　　＜解答＞ is

170. Though Lincoln knew their attitude, he was broad-minded enough to appoint such men to important offices because he was (convinced/convincing) of their ability.

    ＜解答＞ convinced

171. The master's examination consists of two three-hour periods (taken/takes) on consecutive days.

    ＜解答＞ taken

172. These guns shoot large shells, any one of (whom/which) would blow up a house or sink a ship.

    ＜解答＞ which

173. It held their bodies when (their/his) minds refused to go on.

    ＜解答＞ their

174. It was Johnson who, running his tongue (thirstily/thirsty) across his lips, spoke of the reward.

    ＜解答＞ thirstily

175. This gave the Duke of York and the cruisers a chance to close in, then smash and (sink/sank) the Schararnhorst.

    ＜解答＞ sink

176. I'll never be able to explain, not even to myself, just how it (happened/happen).

    ＜解答＞ happened

177. Mamma began pouring wine and passing (them/it) around, stopping only to brush away a tear from time to time.

    ＜解答＞ it

178. Their foliage is more (delicater/delicate) and feathery than that of the other conifers.

    ＜解答＞ delicate

179. The varied classes of organic compounds with (their/its) basically common pattern as well as with their peculiarities and reactions serve as groundwork for this course.

    ＜解答＞ their

180. When the women leaders (held/hold) their first national convention for omen's rights in 1848, they issued the Declaration of Sentiments, demanding equal rights with men in education, economic opportunities, law, and franchise.

　　＜解答＞ held

181. In the rise of the common man during the (nineteenth/nineteen) century, the objective was not merely to secure political privilege but also economic advantages for the underdog.

　　＜解答＞ nineteenth

182. Thomas Hunter (arrived/arrives) in New York in 1850 as a penniless and friendless political fugitive from Ireland.

　　＜解答＞ arrived

183. The people of the well-settled towns on the East coast (was/were) constantly swept by waves of enthusiasm to migrate into the western wilderness, looking for bigger and better opportunities.

　　＜解答＞ were

184. Capital in the form of money or securities is very (carefully/careful) guarded.

　　＜解答＞ carefully

185. In the early (intelligence/intelligent) tests, it was possible for a person to get a good mark if he knew enough root words, suffixes, prefixes.

　　＜解答＞ intelligence

186. By learning all the roots and basic words, and learning how to take a word apart to (determining/determine) its real meaning, you can improve your English.

　　＜解答＞ determine

187. The newness of America can be (seen /see) from historical chronology, but more obviously from personal experience.

　　＜解答＞ seen

188. In fact, a hundred cities and a thousand towns that now stand (proudly/proud) in many parts of the country were carved out of forests and wilderness by the fathers or grand-fathers of living Americans.

<解答>　proudly

189.　The forces mentioned above have not only unified the people of numerous origins but (having/have) also produced an American with distinct characteristics.

<解答>　have

190.　The buffalo was wantonly killed, until (they/it) became almost extinct.

<解答>　it

191.　Even though San Francisco's harder is a splendid one, few harbors in the world are as fine and large (as Rio de Janeiro/as those of Rio de Janeiro).

<解答>　as those of Rio de Janeiro

192.　If I (would have/had) been there, I could have helped you.

<解答>　had

193.　The Graduate Division Office is (normal/normally) a graduate student's first source of information about study for a master's degree.

<解答>　normally

194.　Just as I finished eating, my brother (asked/explained) me a question.

<解答>　asked

195.　On Sunday, after visiting other (interesting/interested) parts of the city, Marie will go to the airport and fly home.

<解答>　interesting

196.　Sixty-seven women have served in the U.S. Congress since the first woman (was elected/elected) in 1916.

<解答>　was elected

197.　An important step was (taken/took) in 1955 when the AFL and CIO were united as the American Federation of Labor and Congress of Industrial Organizations.

<解答>　taken

198.　While the modern scientist's search may be as useless as Eos' wish, it is wiser in that it (seeks/seek) for enduring youth rather than endless life.

<解答>　seeks

199. Few of us (realizes/realize) what a vast amount of information has been gathered about our feathered friends the birds.
    <解答> realize

200. Although these girls had always lived in ideal camping country, they had never (camped/camp) before.
    <解答> camped

201. Once a tropical cyclone is found, these hurricane-hunters risk (his/their) lives to bore through howling wind and hamering rain to the very center of a hurricane.
    <解答> their

202. I wondered if I looked as funny to him as he (did/does) to me.
    <解答> did

203. It seemed that, at the moment the great whale came to the surface to take a breath, the air rushed into (them/it) as if into great machine.
    <解答> it

204. Quickly John took off his shoes, jumped into the water, and started swimming toward the (drowning/drown) man.
    <解答> drowning

205. Grown boys and girls must not (be/are) mollycoddled any more.
    <解答> be

206. The truth is that both science (or/and) nature are difficult.
    <解答> and

207. To many scientists this new uncertainty was (profound/profoundly) disheartening.
    <解答> profoundly

208. And so mathematicians like Rusell became convinced that the symbols in equations need not have (verbal/verb) meaning.
    <解答> verbal

209. These two discoveries, Heisenberg's principle and Goedel's proof, are barriers that human (beings/being) can never hope to vault.
    <解答> beings

210. The second general type of material is openly sold or (exhibited/exhibiting) and endeavors to stay within, but just within, the law.
     <解答> exhibited

211. One day he came to New York and told me about what he (had/has) done.
     <解答> had

212. American education has been regarded as an instrument by which society can build (its/their) own future.
     <解答> its

213. When I was (growing/grown) up, I spent every summer helping out on my grandparents' farm.
     <解答> growing

214. Of course, there are other motives than mere (filth/filthy) money.
     <解答> filthy

215. Second, your school boards (rise/raise) their own money by direct taxes, or at least the greater part of it.
     <解答> raise

216. I am sure that your system seems as odd to us as ours (does/do) to you.
     <解答> does

217. This surprises the proprietor who is behind the bar; he (decides/decide) to give them the best wine in the house.
     <解答> decides

218. How, then, do we measure what a student has accomplished if we (couldn't/can't) count up the number of courses he has satisfactorily taken ?
     <解答> can't

219. It took great effort, since he had a clumsy body to (begun/begin) with, to become a fine first baseman.
     <解答> begin

220. In an effort to expand the improved services of libraries to the public, a new concept of cooperative services (has/have) been developed.
     <解答> has

221. Some people think ants follow each other by (their/its) sense of smell.

 　　＜解答＞ their

222. When Robin arrived on the bank of a stream, he (heard/hears) Friar Tuck humming merrily near by.

 　　＜解答＞ heard

223. The change has often been made against American writers that they do not describe society, and (has/have) no interest in it.

 　　＜解答＞ have

224. This country is worth fighting for, among other reasons, because I know of no other country in which this debate could have (taken/took) place.

 　　＜解答＞ taken

225. The Americans had a greater tendency to name places for people (that/who) had the Spanish ancestors.

 　　＜解答＞ who

226. His emergence into the mainstream of politics has been without (his/its) hazards.

 　　＜解答＞ its

227. In every direction I was pulled and pushed and (greet/greeted) with noisy acclaimations and upspeakable unrest.

 　　＜解答＞ greeted

228. Crabs eat coconut, fish eat (alive/lively) coral, and rats live in the tops of tall trees.

 　　＜解答＞ lively

229. In California, John has a small windowless labortory (that/which) carefully guards his secret.

 　　＜解答＞ which

230. The riots were finally stilled not only by force (but/and) by intercession of the political leadership that Negroes themselves had elected.

 　　＜解答＞ but

231. The interjection is not (really/real) a part of speech.

　　＜解答＞　really

232. There (has/have) been more definitions of the sentence than we can profitally list here.

　　＜解答＞　have

233. The mind of the (commonly/common) man was awake in the world as it had never been before in all the experience of mankind.

　　＜解答＞　common

234. The were now educated men, but how could they put to any purpose (his/their) training and intelligence.

　　＜解答＞　their

235. Unless it is being dramatized or read aloud over the radio, fiction is one of the private (ones/one).

　　＜解答＞　ones

236. Mr. and Mrs. White live in a city, (owned/own) their home and pay taxes on it.

　　＜解答＞　own

237. When he had finished he hung his picture (besides/beside) those which his boarders had made.

　　＜解答＞　besides

238. The sedimentary rocks do not (lay/lie) neatly stratum above stratum.

　　＜解答＞　lie

239. If he is (clearly/clear) enjoying himself, the chances are his readers will share his enjoyment.

　　＜解答＞　clearly

240. Such (was/were) the predominant land life throught the Mesozoic Age.

　　＜解答＞　was

241. The following night Bill returned quite (late/lately) from work to find his wife lying unconscious beside the phone.

　　＜解答＞　late

《TOEFL 托福文法與構句 下冊》勘誤表

頁數	題數	訂正說明
P7	39	B. The → B. the
P21	180	for omen＇s → for women＇s
P26	234	句首 The → They
P27	242	a resue → a rescue
P32	292	〈解答〉dask → dash
P32	298	thinging → thinking
P37	347	fo → for
P44	409	tha → the
P61	603	betters → letters
P94	1061	nucle → uncle
P115	1343	know → knew
P117	1371	acoustice → acoustics
P120	1411	A. the family → A. The family
P120	1413	hight → night
P123	1457	foreing → foreign
P132	1565	〈解答〉werre → were
P146	1743	〈解答〉because he → Because he
P148	1765	〈解答〉you → You 大寫
P156	1888	yoy → you
P158	1917	nito → into
P159	1934	an → and

P161	1953	noting → nothing
P190	2327	herat → heart
P218	2665	thoses → those
P221	2695	dreadeddisease → dreaded disease 兩個字要分開
P221	2696	rothing → rotting
P234	2837	childike → childlike
P239	2884	① A. → A 標點符號取消 ② trupet → trumpet
P241	2909	knowledgealbe → knowledgeable

242. The skipper decided to try a resue, but shells (from shores/from shore) batteries forced the submarine to submerge.

    <解答>　from shore

243. There (have been/has been) little snow in Artic areas for a long time because the atmosphere cannot get much moisture from a frozen ocean.

    <解答>　has been

244. The stars awaken a certain reverence in man because though always present, they are beyond (his/your) reach.

    <解答>　his

245. They would come out to attack and then (disappeared/disappear) back into the deep forests, where their opponents were at a disadvantage.

    <解答>　disappear

246. With few exceptions, the cost of the new apartments (depends/depend) on their location and the number of rooms.

    <解答>　depends

247. Ruth had just returned home and (began/begun) to read a magazine when her brother called to say he had arrived at the railroad station.

    <解答>　begun

248. People who can find nothing good to say about others really hurt no one but (themselves/themself).

    <解答>　themselves

249. Because of the accident, Grandmother will forbid my brother and me (to go swimming/from swimming) in the river unless someone agrees to watch us.

    <解答>　to go swimming

250. He was standing quietly when presently a young woman, who had been combing her hair and (watching/watched) him, approached and asked him for directions.

    <解答>　watching

251. Plants of (these/this) type grow best in places where there is a great deal of shade.

<解答> this

252. By the time he was finally captured, the thief had spent (most/almost) all the money he had stolen.

<解答> almost

253. Of all his outdoor activities, Paul likes fishing (best of all/the best), but he doesn't enjoy clearing them afterwards.

<解答> the best

254. All the neighbors commented on how strange it was for the Smiths to have ever (chosen/chose) so ugly a color to paint their house.

<解答> chosen

255. Plants of (this/those) type grow best in places where there is a great deal of shade.

<解答> this

256. Mr. Mathrison went (painstakingly/painstaking) over all the figures to make sure there were no errors in his calculations.

<解答> painstakingly

257. She is one of those persons (which/who) accept whatever may happen and never utter a word of complaint.

<解答> who

258. The more we attemted to explain our mistake, the (worse/worst) our story sounded.

<解答> worse

259. Neither Richard nor I was able to recall when Mary had last (spoke/spoken) to us in so friendly a manner.

<解答> spoken

260. Four different languages were (spoken/spoke) at the conference, but I was unable to understand any of them.

<解答> spoken

261. Although Ronald had certainly not been sickly as a boy, in recent years he had frequently felt (bad/badly).

　　＜解答＞　bad

262. Mrs. Baker asked that she have to go to see the children who (will/would) come to this city tomorrow.

　　＜解答＞　would

263. The cook (has opened/opened) the kitchen window as soon as he could, but the smoke from the scorched roast kept swirling up from the oven.

　　＜解答＞　opened

264. It was been estimated that the efforts of only one per cent of the world's population (moves/move) civilization forward.

　　＜解答＞　move

265. Mrs. Fisher asked that Charles and I talk (more softer/more softly) so as not to wake the children.

　　＜解答＞　more softly

266. After he had (run/ran) almost half a mile, he looked back and saw the tower crumbling.

　　＜解答＞　run

267. Durig his mother's absence, the baby had spilled his milk, broken a dish, and (torn/tore) several pages from the book she had been reading.

　　＜解答＞　torn

268. Not only may such a love have deepened and exalted, (and/but) may still deepen and exalt, the life of any man of any age.

　　＜解答＞　but

269. Why is a man in civil life perpetually slandering and backbiting his fellow men, and (why is he/is) unable to see good even in his friends ?

　　＜解答＞　why is he

270. He said that if any visitor (are/were) to ask, no information should be given.

　　＜解答＞　were

271. In the last decade movie production has advanced (rapidly/forward) with great strides.

　　＜解答＞　rapidly

272. The commission decided to reimburse the property owners, to readjust the states, and (that it would extend/to extend) the services in the near future.

　　＜解答＞　to extend

273. To continue reading the meaning of these sentence will become clear to you and finally, try to avoid going back and (to reread/rereading) words and phrases.

　　＜解答＞　rereading

274. Tom and his brother did not enjoy fishing but (hunting/to hunt) on their vacation.

　　＜解答＞　hunting

275. Even the best drivers car have an accident if (you are/he is) tired and the driving conditions are bad.

　　＜解答＞　he is

276. Besides the store that is opposite (over/to) the road, there is another store selling such goods.

　　＜解答＞　to

277. I would go to visit that beautiful lake but I (couldn't/can't) get in touch with you while I am in Boston.

　　＜解答＞　couldn't

278. They have chosen the kinds of books (that is/that are) fairly popular among the average intelligent readers.

　　＜解答＞　that are

279. My father convinced me that nothing was useful which (was/is) not honest.

　　＜解答＞　was

280. Force yourself to read slightly (more faster/faster) than seems comfortable.

　　＜解答＞　faster

281. In such a large crowd the policeman had considerable difficulty locating the woman (which/who) had called for help.

　　＜解答＞　who

282. The historian found the reading of the ancient manuscripts to be (a/an) agreeable, not a tiresome, occupation.
＜解答＞ an

283. I (sat/set) my suitcase down in front of a hotel shop and ordered a taxi.
＜解答＞ set

284. I never feel (badly/bad) if after trying hard I fail to win a prize; the effort gives me satisfaction.
＜解答＞ bad

285. It is an accepted custom in our country for men to remove their hats when a woman (enters/entered) the room.
＜解答＞ enters

286. Because he was very sick, he (laid/lay) in bed waiting for the doctor to come.
＜解答＞ lay

287. When I stayed in Chicago with my aunt and her children, my aunt used to ask me to rest (immediate/immediately) as soon as she came home.
＜解答＞ immediately

288. Neither the Gold he served nor the learning he preserved counted for much in the world from (where/whom) he had retired.
＜解答＞ where

289. A characteristic of American culture that has become a tradition is the glorification of the self made man, the man who has (rose/risen) to the top through his own efforts, usually beginning by working with his hands.
＜解答＞ risen

290. Members of both the House and Senate Armed Services Committees predicted that Johnson would (rise/raise) the present 525,000 on ceiling of U.S. troops there by 50,000 to 100,000, or extend the current Vietnam tour of duty, or both.
＜解答＞ raise

291. For all the obvious, neither of the Sharpest of the senatorial critics of the Johnson Administration's handling of the incident Wayne Morse and William Fulbright (question/questioned) that some sort of an engagement did take place

on August 4.

＜解答＞ questioned

292. Alice was quietly reading over her sister's shoulder when she saw a white rabbit (dashed/dash) across the lawn and dissappear into its hole.

＜解答＞ dask

293. But when the restraining wire was slipped, the machine started off (very/so) quickly I could stay with it only a few feet.

＜解答＞ so

294. The usual fruit of the interaction between majority (or/and) minority is compromise, and compromise is the heart and soul of the political process.

＜解答＞ and

295. We city dwellers often fail to take advantage of our opportunities of the enjoyments city life (offer/offers).

＜解答＞ offers

296. Left alone, the children have (ate/eaten) all the food that was left in the kitchen.

＜解答＞ eaten

297. The forces mentioned above have not only unified the people of numerous origins but (had/having) also produced an American with distinct characteristics.

＜解答＞ had

298. I took another way to return that had come, thinging I could easily keep enough of the island in sight so that I would not (loose/lost) my way.

＜解答＞ loose

299. No inventor has (yet/already) built a musical instrument to match the ingenious flexibility of the human vocal tract, with its rubbery, marvelously mobil walls.

＜解答＞ yet

300. Of the many improvements to the automobile (itself/themselves), which one was probably the most important ?

＜解答＞ itself

301. The cost of the new cars in this state (were/was) considerably higher than we had expected.

＜解答＞ was

302. Jack had once seen a horse swim the river and (to disappear/disappear) up the narrow box canyon.

＜解答＞ disappear

303. Sometimes I get the idea that a student (is expected/was) to think about getting educated for the sake of society as if he was not a part of it.

＜解答＞ was

304. Unless one (be/is) familiar with journalistic style the techniques used in this essay may not be obvious.

＜解答＞ is

305. Please do not feel bad when you have to (encounter/encounter on) such adverse situation in which you have been engaged.

＜解答＞ encounter

306. A person who cannot be enthusiastic about things won't (get/make) very far in this would.

＜解答＞ get

307. If (one doesn't/you don't) have confidence in yourself so that others will respect you, you cannot expect them to pay attention you.

＜解答＞ you don't

308. Until we receive word that the necessary records (are/is) accessible, we cannot accommodate him by speeding up the procedure.

＜解答＞ are

309. His irrelevant remarks about the stationary machine (was/were) a surprise to all of us.

＜解答＞ were

310. The thief undoubtedly waited for Mr. Baker to go out and entered by the back window and removed the silver without (being/ever been) seen.

＜解答＞ being

311. The committee asked the sheriff (corroborate/to corroborate) the report that the assistant superintendent did not succeed in his vicious plan to tyrannize.

<解答>　to corroborate

312. (Because/Because of) his absence he did not hear the professor analyze the description of the ballon; therefore, he was not conscious of his mistakes in grammar.

<解答>　Because of

313. The lawyer (who/which) defended the driver of the second car had himself been a victim of similar accident the previous year.

<解答>　who

314. Ecstasy is sometimes desirable, and exhilaration (overcomes/overcome) despair; but either can exceed good taste and cause the development of a dilemma.

<解答>　overcomes

315. The irritable sergeant was insistant that nothing (supersedes/supersede) the drilling of the forty new men.

<解答>　supersede

316. Sheriff Brown felt bad when he was compelled to arrest Mr. Smith, his neighbor, who he knew, was (a/an) honest man in this city.

<解答>　an

317. There (is/are) no Daily Specials, but the prices are remarkably low.

<解答>　are

318. Because his study covered only 1000 persons Solomon is careful about estimating how many overweight persons in the population (has/have) metabolic disturbances.

<解答>　have

319. What happened in Los Angeles (were/was) an explosion of violence against autority by those who had been left behind in our modern industrial society.

<解答>　was

320. I grew thin and so depressed that, (be/being) a good Catholic, I at last carried my troubles to my priest.

    <解答> being

321. Perhaps the easiest and simplest and, hence, the most common form of entertianment outside the home (is/are) going to the movies.

    <解答> is

322. These little girl lay on the floor without protest after eating lunch for their mother have (learned/taught) them to take a nap after lunch.

    <解答> taught

323. If you (had known/knew) many pieces John ate for breakfast this morning, you would never have doubted why he is overweight.

    <解答> had known

324. One of the workers has hung the curtains that had been (laying/laid) on the floor.

    <解答> laid

325. Thanks to the various internatal exchange programs, continentals between universities (almost disappeared/have almost been disappeared).

    <解答> almost disappeared

326. Considerably higher on the smoothed rock appear fourteen figures in precisely the same style (like/as) those at the Tuckte, Jum sheed.

    <解答> as

327. I carried the box to the room where I lived, set it down with care in the closet, laid the key on it, and (locked/locking) the closet.

    <解答> locked

328. She told me long before his last illness that I should expect nothing from my uncle, who (is/was) my father's brother.

    <解答> was

329. No doubt you have always had expectations, and I desire that you continue (to expect/expect).

    <解答> to expect

330. You should make the other fellow (to feel/feel) important, if you want to get along with him and have him like you, because that is the way to do it.

    ＜解答＞ feel

331. Dr. Martin became very impatient and phoned the post office to ask why (there was/it was) no mail delivery.

    ＜解答＞ there was

332. The senator, with his clerks and secretaries, (draw/draws) a whacking salary from the treasury every week.

    ＜解答＞ draws

333. Mr. Henry Green felt very (badly/bad) because Edith and I had to ask whomever we had known in Philadelphia to cooperate toward the common end.

    ＜解答＞ bad

334. He also told of (frightening/frightened) events that had taken place in his native state of Connecticut and listed the fearful things he had seen on his nightly walks in sleepy hollow.

    ＜解答＞ frightening

335. Every morning Johnny would go to the park, swing on the swing, (run/running) around the baseball diamond, and climb up.

    ＜解答＞ run

336. Joan is one of those people who think that rivers are (more prettier/prettier) than lakes.

    ＜解答＞ prettier

337. Although I have lived in this country (since/after) last September, I still have trouble getting used to American food.

    ＜解答＞ since

338. Those of (us/them) who wear glasses should have their eyes examined at regular intervals.

    ＜解答＞ them

339. After barely tasting the food, the old woman called the waiter to her table and complained that everything tasted (bad/badly)

 ＜解答＞ bad

340. On their way to work each morning, several day-maids take the same bus I (do/did).

 ＜解答＞ do

341. Mary found it difficult to talk (calm/calmly) about what she had experienced at the station.

 ＜解答＞ camly

342. The members of the children's orchestra were told that when one is asked to play more softly, (you/he) should not play loudly.

 ＜解答＞ he

343. A drop in spending together with a boost in prices (has/have) caused a mild recession.

 ＜解答＞ has

344. The wounded man (laid/lay) in the street for over an hour before the ambulance arrived.

 ＜解答＞ lay

345. Alan Kleinwax expects you and (I/me) to come to the Lincoln Studio to have our pictures taken tomorrow at ten.

 ＜解答＞ me

346. The manager of the Social Security Office, with his assistants and secretaries, (are/is) coming to check over your payroll today.

 ＜解答＞ is

347. Williams sold his apartment house at a (fairly/fair) higher price than he had paid fo it.

 ＜解答＞ fairly

348. The merchant knew how to flatter his customers and display his wares (well/good), but he was notorious for his cheating.

 ＜解答＞ well

349. Paul would go to the old barn, catch birds, (throw/throwing) stones into the pond, or pound the trunks of trees with a stick till they resounded like drums.
　　＜解答＞　throw

350. (Despite of/In spite of) all the snow in the valley, the cabin remained warm and comfortable.
　　＜解答＞　In spite of

351. The opinion of all the students interviewed (seems/seem) to be that the food in local restaurants in getting worse day by day.
　　＜解答＞　seems

352. Cowboys in movies never seem to have any trouble drawing guns (out of/out from) their holsters.
　　＜解答＞　out of

353. There were some cakes in the kitchen but Jean wanted to have that (more smaller/smaller) one of the two cakes.
　　＜解答＞　smaller

354. In this country it is asked that any one who has recently come here (have/has) to pay the tax.
　　＜解答＞　have

355. Before people had (either/neither) or a business system that produced goods and services, they traded goods for goods.
　　＜解答＞　either

356. An Englishman traveling in Africa once (offered/offers) iron to a native tribe in exchange for a canoe.
　　＜解答＞　offered

357. I would surely go over there to meet you in New York, when you had completed your college courses and (began/begun) to leave for home in November.
　　＜解答＞　begun

358. If you were to ask Jim what (did he/he did) with his money, he would have difficulty remembering .

<解答> he did

359. How many times have you spent money for one thing and then wished later
    you (have/had) kept it for something else ?
    <解答> had

360. Books that have been compiled for the express purpose of (giving out/to give
    out) information are called reference book.
    <解答> giving out

361. With John and (I/me) going to see Professor Baker and to convince him to
    accept our suggestions we will have no difficulty winning him.
    <解答> me

362. Dictionaries vary in size from one small enough (to carry/carry) in your pocket
    to the very large unabridged dictionary that you can scarcely lift.
    <解答> to carry

363. Not too many years ago, it was an (excited/exciting) experience to travel 25 or
    50 miles from home.
    <解答> exciting

364. He asked me what I was doing when he (called/calls).
    <解答> called

365. The first explanation is that the weight of the hill has (compressed/compress)
    ammonia in the depths of the ground and that the escaping ammonia freezes
    the water as in the manufacture of artificial ice.
    <解答> compressed

366. Now if these wonder lads of baseball could win over the team from La Mesa,
    California, they (would/will) become Little League World Champions.
    <解答> would

367. As soon as possible after the student begins his graduate (training/trained), he
    should present a prospectus for his master's thesis.
    <解答> training

368. Here the distance and direction of the target from the sun (are/is) calculated by
    almost automatic machines.

<解答> are

369. When they asked for Professor MacDonald and found him to be a wrinkled little man in a greasy white suit, there (were/was) a joy in them, for a moment, which rose above their other feelings: the pride of a thing shored.
<解答> was

370. Was it another (man/men) who had been lost in the middle of the ocean ?
<解答> man

371. The Sunday evenings are once again as before, except that Angelina has married Dick, and now he also (is/are) with us every Sunday.
<解答> is

372. In this course the students become more (familiarly/familiar) with the essence of scientific methods and explore the intrinsic mechanism of physical-chemical processes.
<解答> familiar

373. Though (this/these) little things are interesting and significant they by no means encompass the whole scope of Mrs. Roosevelt's public activities.
<解答> these

374. She was (teld/told) by women that they had husbands to protect their rights and that what she needed was a husband.
<解答> told

375. Men of more than average ability could, of course, take advantage (of/in) the bigger opportunities.
<解答> of

376. At the age of thirteen, he had to leave public school and (take/took) a job as office boy in a telegraph company.
<解答> take

377. Most educators believe that some common goals should be (set/sat) for all students in college.
<解答> set

378. Curiously enough, the vacabulary part of a test is one of the easiest to beat if you make a (determined/determine) effort to learn words systematically.
    ＜解答＞ determined

379. Modern tests (contains/contain) words which are more difficult to guess at.
    ＜解答＞ contain

380. At that time the old lady (is/was) ninety-six, but she still remembered that when she was twenty-five years old.
    ＜解答＞ was

381. Thus both the South and (the West/West) are developing into industrial regions.
    ＜解答＞ the West

382. The American (is/are) not merely confident but is ambitious and loves freedom and independence.
    ＜解答＞ is

383. This wholesale destruction of wild life has upset the balance (in/of) nature.
    ＜解答＞ of

384 In other words, nature seems to have reversed (it/him) by freezing water into ice in the summer and melting the ice in winter.
    ＜解答＞ it

385. The responsibility to the general public on the part of these corporations and their subsidiaries (is/are) not lessened by the fact that they pay heavy taxes.
    ＜解答＞ is

386. Bishop had (ridden/rode) in a day coach all the way from New York and was very tired when he arrived in Jacksonville.
    ＜解答＞ ridden

387. After she has breakfast, her friends are going to drive her to the (historical/history) towards of Concord and Lexington.
    ＜解答＞ historical

388. When Henry Allen came home from the office last Thursday night he saw a note from his wife on the (kitchen/kitchens) table.
    ＜解答＞ kitchen

389. Attempts (was/were) made to form trade unions soon after the United States became a nation.

　　＜解答＞ were

390. The fear of growing old has been common to every race and every age and (led/has led) men on strange quests.

　　＜解答＞ has led

391. Occasionally, like soup in an over-full pot, its contents overflowed slightly, running down (its/their) sides and spreading out for a short distance toward the other cones.

　　＜解答＞ its

392. Also by radio waves you may fry eggs on a stove that never gets (hot/hotly) enough to burn paper or burn you if you should touch it.

　　＜解答＞ hot

393. A great sheet of flame belches from its mouth and the hot blast of the gun can be (felt/feel) for hundreds of feet.

　　＜解答＞ felt

394. They did a lot of funny things and made the children laugh and (clap/clapping) their hands.

　　＜解答＞ clap

395. They agreed because he was a (died/dying) man and they respected him.

　　＜解答＞ dying

396. They were always discussing the chances of a meeting, watching (closely/close) the vast surface of the ocean.

　　＜解答＞ closely

397. The directions for this kind of exercise at first glance seem (needlessly/needless) complex.

　　＜解答＞ needlessly

398. New truths (exposed/expose) today in the explosive growth of modern science cannot wait centuries for appreciation.

　　＜解答＞ exposed

399. Until early in the nineteenth century, mathematics was based on sets of axioms and postulates that (was/were) considered self-evident.
    ＜解答＞ were

400. Making sequences of symbols that are not significant but rigorously logical is far more difficult (than/with) it sounds.
    ＜解答＞ than

401. Let me give you two of the consequences, of which I would guess that one will shock you, while (another/the other) may perhaps surprise you more favorably.
    ＜解答＞ the other

402. As soon as the child goes to school, he is quickly aware of how important it is to be (thought/think) well of.
    ＜解答＞ thought

403. But the pressure of numbers (in/upon) school is such that a stupid boy or girl will have great difficulty getting in.
    ＜解答＞ upon

404. The mother decided that the children could go for a quick swim, but (they should be/be) back no later than six o'clock.
    ＜解答＞ they should be

405. Mary said that she would (neither/either) go to visit her uncle in Chicago or see her brother in New York.
    ＜解答＞ either

406. This phenomenon has (been described/described) so often as to need no further cliches on the subject here.
    ＜解答＞ been described

407. Scientists are searching for the oldest tree (lively/alive) because it can teach them a great deal about many matters.
    ＜解答＞ alive

408. For the highly specialized scholar, it should soon be possible for him to request and receive special information (stored/storing) anywhere around the world.
    ＜解答＞ stored

409. President Lincoln, walking with a friend, turned back to assist a beetle that (lie/lay) on its back, legs clawing tha air, vainly trying to turn itself over.
＜解答＞ lay

410. The academic community is as free to pursue them (as/like) any other group of citizens, but no freer.
＜解答＞ as

411. As many congressman interpreted the message, the president was feeling even more (generous/generously) than he seemed.
＜解答＞ generous

412. You forget to be sensitive about the situation very (quickly/quick).
＜解答＞ quickly

413. A score of years ago, a friend (placed/places) in my hand a book called " True Peace. "
＜解答＞ placed

414. A break of just one link in that chain have (meant/mean) a watery grave for all behind the break.
＜解答＞ meant

415. Bees are (exposed/exposing) to many hardship and many dangers.
＜解答＞ exposed

416. We are not (particular/particularly) aware of idioms until we begin to study a foreign language.
＜解答＞ particularly

417. One possible definition of grammar is that it is a descriptive and, (in/to) a large extent, a prescriptive scheme for this word interplay.
＜解答＞ to

418. After a thorough inspection of the Babylonian tables, he predicted that another eclipse of the sun was due (in/on) May 28, 585 B.C.
＜解答＞ on

419. It seemed indecent that I had consumed enough canned food to have (left/leaved) this tremendous pile.

<解答> left

420. But all spider, and especially hairy ones, have an (extremely/extreme) delicate sense of touch.

<解答> extremely

421. You don't discover what should go into your novel by taking a poll or (having/have) a trial run in Boston or Philadelphia.

<解答> having

422. Strangers (coming/come) into her city now notice what a clean place it is.

<解答> coming

423. As we draw near, the ship shivers when the captain fires the harpoon gun (which/that) drives the harpoon deep into the whale.

<解答> that

424. Now scientific men are not able to explain to us either why offspring should resemble (or/not) why they should differ from their parents.

<解答> or

425. Probably man (alone/along) could never have maintained the fallacy of masculine incapacity without the aid of women.

<解答> alone

426. Almost every morning I receive cards inviting me to art exphibitions, and on the cards (were/had been) photographs of the works exhibited.

<解答> were

427. Columbus in the Santa Maria and the Pilgrims in the Mayflower traveled (comfortably/comfortable) compared with Dr. Hannes Indemann on his journey.

<解答> comfortably

428. The good statesman, like all sensible human beings, always learns more from (their/his) exponents than from supporters.

<解答> his

429. The dancers were told that no one should think too high of (himself/themselves).

<解答> himself

430. It seemed impossible for either of us to remain; for both she and I (have/had) to be present at another meeting.

    <解答> had

431. After searching, the police concluded that the thief had come in through the window and (had stolen/stole) the silver dish.

    <解答> had stolen

432. The policeman allows people to stay but he does not (let/leave) them enter easily.

    <解答> let

433. His hopes (to make/of making) a great future with the cotton gin were never realized.

    <解答> of making

434. If it (were not/had not been) for the knowledge he gained from Gilbert's expeditions, Raleigh would probably have been far less successful in his explorations of the American coasts.

    <解答> had not been

435. Although I have the highest personal regard for Frofessor Baker, I must confess that I find (little/few) major points in this book to which he and I agree.

    <解答> few

436. In order to make people change their feeling about his writer, he has to write another (books/book) regarding this problem.

    <解答> book

437. I don't know the person (who/whom) talked with you in the street when you were waiting for the bus.

    <解答> who

438. Jack Ball has seen many cutting (human hair/human hairs) and these people appear to be interested in this practice.

    <解答> human hair

439. It is easier to have the best tool than it is to use (them/it).
　　＜解答＞ it

440. Everyone in the delegation had (his/their) reason for opposing the measure.
　　＜解答＞ his

441. He was standing quietly when presently a young woman, who had been coming her hair and (watching/watched) him, approached and asked him for directions.
　　＜解答＞ watching

442. In our school the teachers would leave most students (to go/go) out early on Friday afternoons before football games.
　　＜解答＞ to go

443. Since he is not as sociable as his brother, he has fewer friends (as/than) his brother.
　　＜解答＞ than

444. The new of the Josses suffered by our troops (was/were) much worse than expected.
　　＜解答＞ was

445. Professor Baker invited me to visit him on his farm a few weeks ago, and I went there on time to find out that he (sat/set) down near his garden reading a book.
　　＜解答＞ sat

446. If he (had known/knew) about contemporay politics, he would have been willing to use it as his pretext for speech.
　　＜解答＞ had known

447. Profound changes such as these go forwaed (rapid/rapidly) in the social and economic spheres, whereas the arts remain cautious, conservative, and European.
　　＜解答＞ rapidly

448. No one on the committee had flatly made (some/any) such allegations, though Wayne Morse did come close by declaring that the U.S. had provoked the

North Vietnamese.

＜解答＞ any

449. His trip was (largely/large) political in nature, but, because he was an excellent businessman, his perception of what the world might be in the postwar years was strongly tinged with business insights.

＜解答＞ largely

450. Lincoln reached Washington at six o'clock on February 23, but word of his arrival was (keep/kept) secret until after the train from Harrisbung had reached Baltimore.

＜解答＞ kept

451. With all the knowledge and skill (acquired/acquiring) in thousands of flights in the last ten years, I would hardly think today of making my first flight on a strange machine in twenty-seven-mile wind.

＜解答＞ acquired

452. Of all the will for the ideal (which/who) exists in mankind only a small part can be manifested in action.

＜解答＞ which

453. Sometimes an irresistible and persistent conscience (causes/cause) one to discriminate against himself and to pursue duty in panicky way.

＜解答＞ causes

454. This is the story of (mine/my) coming to the beautiful Black Hills, where I have since lived and hope to live for the rest of my life.

＜解答＞ my

455. My next difficulty was to make a sieve (separate/to separate) the grain from the husk.

＜解答＞ separate

456. As I have indicated above, rapid increase in world population imposes a severe burden on efforts to (rise/raise) levels of living.

＜解答＞ raise

457. This passenger was asked to pay (a/an) extra sum of money an account of the unpredicatable spendings.
　　＜解答＞ an

458. " I'll show you my snapshots if (you'll show/you show) me yours." Said Judy's sister Jill.
　　＜解答＞ you show

459. Nobody who will not try to help the other people develop (his/their) abilities deserves to have friends.
　　＜解答＞ their

460. The dessert has been flavored with an ingredient low in calories, but it tastes as (sweet/sweetly) as though it had sugar in it.
　　＜解答＞ sweet

461. It is all right for one to be changeable, but (they/one) must be colly aware that no one is indispensable and that to disappoint one's friends is foolish.
　　＜解答＞ one

462. We shall describe no more of these monuments, although several (exists/exist) in various parts of the kingdom and possibly some may have escaped the inquiries of travellers.
　　＜解答＞ exist

463. The peasant who live in these villages first (have/has) to put a lot from their khan and build a house of it.
　　＜解答＞ have

464. The argument about the category of the food had not (achieved/achieve) anything except the embarrassment of connoisseur.
　　＜解答＞ achieved

465. Watching the pendulum oscillate in mythical fashion (as/like) a weird pastime.
　　＜解答＞ like

466. All these incidents are (more nearer/nearer) to the people of Midwest than to those of eastern seaboard.

<解答> nearer

467. In the long run cafeterias are always cheaper (to/than) restaurants because you do not have to tip waitresses.

<解答> than

468. The landlady (suspected/suspicioned) that someone must have broken into the house while she was watching the T.V. show.

<解答> suspected

469. It was (her/she) who shaped the education of her children, she who took her daughter and two sons abroad and put them in school in Paris where they learned to speak fluent French.

<解答> she

470. Two years (have/has) passed, and I am one of the richest men in the city, yet have no more money as will keep me alive.

<解答> has

471. Still holding the young man's hand he paused, and then added deliberately: Now I am not the man to let a cause (be/to be) lost for want of a word.

<解答> be

472. Ross was opposed to this action, but the lieutenant that they continue (to do/do) everything possible to obtain help.

<解答> to do

473. His hostess did not tell him that the girl had come in from the field and (run/ran) hurriedly upstairs so that her foe would not see what she actually did see in the girl's eyes.

<解答> run

474. The child born on April 27, 1822 to Mr. and Mrs. Jesse Grant of Point Pleasant, Ohio, was six weeks old before a name (was found/found) for him.

<解答> was found

475. Neither in his campaign (nor in/nor) his acceptable speech did Mr. Miles acknowledge those whose assistance had won him the nomination.

<解答> nor in

476. A person ought not to forget to use tact and courtesy in dealing with others, if he expects them (to like/like) him and be his friends.

    ＜解答＞ to like

477. It I (had/should) not watched Mrs. Lin, she would have gone without food herself in order to feed the refugees.

    ＜解答＞ had

478. Of those who have visited Rockford, Illinois, with Margaret and (he/him) Ellen is the only one that has shown friendly attitude.

    ＜解答＞ him

479. The problems facing the Minister of France cannot be ignored without (their endangering/they endanger) the stability of the economy.

    ＜解答＞ their endangering

480. Given his choice of the two cakes, johnny regarded them thoughtfully for a moment and then chose the (smaller/smallest) one.

    ＜解答＞ smaller

481. Robert always does whatever he pleases, without regard (of/to) the feelings of others.

    ＜解答＞ to

482. Miss Green asked that each student leave (his/their) paper on the desk, upon completing the day's assignment.

    ＜解答＞ his

483. As the world's population continues to grow, the production of all kinds of foodstuffs (is/are) constantly being made more difficult.

    ＜解答＞ is

484. " Poverty is a psychological process which destroys the young before (he/they) can live and the aged before they can die, " says Yale Psychologist Ira Goldenberg.

    ＜解答＞ they

485. I should insist that he (be not/will not be) accepted as a member since he is very bad-tempered.

<解答> be not

486. Aside from the most important speech he had made before Virginia Legislature, Henry urged the people of the State (to help/help) the northern colonies in their fight.

<解答> to help

487. We understand that Allen is one of the students who (has/have) made the most of the opportunity to study abroad.

<解答> have

488. It isn't proper to complain about his integrity, his probity and his (being impartial/impartiality) in dealing with such a case.

<解答> impartiality

489. He has a hard time (studying/to study) English.

<解答> studying

490. A number of the pictures (are/is) excellent.

<解答> are

491. Write your composition (in/with) ink.

<解答> in

492. We feel grateful (to/for) his help.

<解答> for

493. When all the students (were seated/seated), the professor began his lecture.

<解答> were seated

494. He would gain weight but he (doesn't eat/didn't eat).

<解答> doesn't eat

495. The victim of the accident sued the bus company for (damages/damage).

<解答> damages

496. Please lock the door when you (leave/will leave).

<解答> leave

497. Forty miles on that road (seems/seem) like two hundred.

<解答> seems

498. How many pages (have you studied/did you study) ?

<解答>　have you studied

499. I wish I (hadn't/hadn't had) a cold last night.

<解答>　hadn't had

500. If you had told me in advance, I (would have met/would had met) him.

<解答>　would have met

501. It is necessary that we (go/going) immediately because something may happen here at any time.

<解答>　go

502. It is not the words that matter (so much as/as much as) the way you say them.

<解答>　so much as

503. If Jean had come, I (would have given/would give) her that money.

<解答>　would have given

504. My pen is used out, may I (lend yours/borrow yours) ?

<解答>　borrow yours

505. If it (rains/would rain) tomorrow, I think I'll attend the meeting.

<解答>　rains

506. I want everything (ready/to ready) by two o'clock.

<解答>　ready

507. My mother made me (visit/visited) my relatives before I came to college.

<解答>　visit

508. That's very hard to say, but I wish I (had studied/studied) psychology when I was a college student.

<解答>　had studied

509. I (would explain/will explain) to him if I thought he would understand.

<解答>　would explain

510. If you (had listened/listen) to me, we wouldn't be in danger.

<解答>　had listened

511. If I (had/would) been there, I could have helped you.

<解答>　had

512. (Do/Would) you like to eat your breakfast in the morning ?

    ＜解答＞ Would

513. He said that he (would/will) come to see you next year.

    ＜解答＞ would

514. I won't wait for you, but I will see you (finish/to finish) that work.

    ＜解答＞ finish

515. He has his temperature (taking/taken) in the hospital.

    ＜解答＞ taken

516. They have been waiting for many hours to see the movie stars, but the plane must have been (on time/behind schedule).

    ＜解答＞ behind schedule

517. I don't like to eat at this restaurant, the waiter gave me a steak (rarely cooked/cooked rarely).

    ＜解答＞ rarely cooked

518. The church (lies/lays) north of the town, have you been there ?

    ＜解答＞ lies

519. Jean looked like her father, and she (takes/looks) after her mother in personality.

    ＜解答＞ takes

520. During the exam, we are permitted to talk, walk, or smoke. That's right. The school authority won't allow (to smoke/smoking).

    ＜解答＞ smoking

521. What will you be doing by the time your sister returns home ? I (shall be/shall have been) to Chicago for my summer vacation.

    ＜解答＞ shall have been

522. As you know, my schoolmates never (hanged/hung) their clothes well.

    ＜解答＞ hung

523. He didn't, because John said that the floor was (so/such) crowded that he couldn't dance.

    ＜解答＞ so

524. Why didn't you visit your mother on the farm in the States ? I was very busy, but I know I (had to/should have) at that time.
＜解答＞ should have

525. What would you have done if you (hadn't had/didn't have) to work yesterday.
＜解答＞ hadn't had

526. After the funeral, the residents of the apartment building sent flowers (faithful/faithfully) to the cemetery each week.
＜解答＞ faithfully

527. The committee has met and (they/it) has reached a decision.
＜解答＞ it

528. John's score on the test is the highest in the class; he (must have/had) studied last night.
＜解答＞ must have

529. Florida has not yet ratified the Equal Rights Amendment, and (neither/either) have several other states.
＜解答＞ neither

530. California relies heavily on income from fruit crops, and (does so/so does) Florida.
＜解答＞ so does

531. This year will be difficult for this organization because it has (less/little) money and fewer volunteers than it had last year.
＜解答＞ less

532. There has not been a great response to the sale, (hasn't there/has there) ?
＜解答＞ has there

533. Because the first pair of pants did not fit properly, he asked for (another pair/another pants).
＜解答＞ another pair

534. Alfred Adams has not ever lived alone (before/ago).
＜解答＞ before

535. After (entering/entered) the new school he began to make friends more easily.
     ＜解答＞ entering

536. It is very difficult to stop the cultivation of marijiuana because it (grew/grows) well with little care.
     ＜解答＞ grows

537. Many of the current international problems we are now (face/facing) are the result of misunderstandings.
     ＜解答＞ facing

538. John said that no other car could go as fast as (his/my) car.
     ＜解答＞ his

539. While (attempt/attempting) to reach his home before the storm, John had an accident on his bicycle.
     ＜解答＞ attempting

540. The changes in this city have occurred (fastly/rapidly).
     ＜解答＞ rapidly

541. It was not until she had arrived home (that/when) she remembered her appointment with the doctor.
     ＜解答＞ that

542. George would certainly have attended the proceedings (has/had) he not had a flat tire.
     ＜解答＞ had

543. (Never have so many women/Never so many women have) received law degrees as today.
     ＜解答＞ Never have so many women

544. The students liked that professor's course because there was little or (not/no) homework.
     ＜解答＞ no

545. George knew (how/how to) he could improve his test scores, but he did not have enough time to studay.
     ＜解答＞ how

546. If Mike had (being/been) able to finish his homework he would have come to class.
     ＜解答＞ been

547. Lee contributed fifty dollars, but he wishes he could contribute (another fifty/one other fifty dollars).
     ＜解答＞ another fifty

548. The people at the party were worried about Janet because on one was aware (where that/of where) she had gone.
     ＜解答＞ of where

549. Nancy hasn't begun working her Ph. D. (yet/still) because she is still working on her master's.
     ＜解答＞ yet

550. The director of this organization must know how to manage money, sell his product, and (satisfy/satisfied) the stockholders.
     ＜解答＞ satisfy

551. The cyclist (has/had) looked cautiously before he crossed the main street.
     ＜解答＞ had

552. Here (is/are) the notebook and report that I promised you last week.
     ＜解答＞ are

553. Neither Jane nor her brothers (need/needs) a consent form tomorrow's field trip.
     ＜解答＞ need

554. The skiers would rather (traveling/travel) by train through the mountains than go by bus.
     ＜解答＞ travel

555. Pioneer men and women endured terrible hardships, and (so/so did) their children.
     ＜解答＞ so did

556. Mr. Duncan does not know (where they put/they put where) the lawn mower after they had finished using it.

　　　　　　＜解答＞　where they put

557.　Our flight from Ansterdam to London was delayed (because of/because) the heavy fog.

　　　　　　＜解答＞　because of

558.　Of the two new teachers, one is experienced and (another is inexperienced/the other is not).

　　　　　　＜解答＞　the other is not

559.　George belongs to the (upper middle/high medium) class.

　　　　　　＜解答＞　upper middle

560.　They asked him (don't give/not to give) that new information to anyone else but the sergeant.

　　　　　　＜解答＞　not ot give

561.　John has not been able to recall where (did she live/she lives).

　　　　　　＜解答＞　she lives

562.　Those students do not like to read novels (in any case/much less) text books.

　　　　　　＜解答＞　much less

563.　All who have taken the test are to (sit/set) on the back seats.

　　　　　　＜解答＞　sit

564.　Much care must be taken of new plants when they are first (set/sit).

　　　　　　＜解答＞　set

565.　As we came nearer, the big cat (sprang/sprung) from a limb over our heads.

　　　　　　＜解答＞　sprang

566.　He has been told many times to (lie/lay) and rest.

　　　　　　＜解答＞　lie

567.　Time after time he fell from the high rope, but at last he learned to (catch/caught) the swing.

　　　　　　＜解答＞　catch

568.　These people no longer ate their enemies, but they (fought/fight) every other group that they met.

　　　　　　＜解答＞　fought

569. Harry had (drawn/drawed) all of the pictures without consulting the book.
     ＜解答＞ drawn

570. Giant trees, dripping with moss, (grow/grows) there.
     ＜解答＞ grow

571. (Is/Are) one of the girls bringing your luggage ?
     ＜解答＞ Is

572. There (live/lives) the old man and his wife.
     ＜解答＞ live

573. Several (uses/use) the same locker for books.
     ＜解答＞ use

574. Sue, with her playmates, (plays/play) all day long.
     ＜解答＞ plays

575. Either apples or pears (was/were) served.
     ＜解答＞ were

576. Neither her aunt nor her cousins (speak/speaks) well for her.
     ＜解答＞ speak

577. Neither of the houses (has/have) a new paint job.
     ＜解答＞ has

578. There (is/are) few trolley care left in the cities.
     ＜解答＞ are

579. There fourths of our pledges (were/was) collected.
     ＜解答＞ were

580. Ten tons (is/are) clipped every time with the shovel.
     ＜解答＞ is

581. Everyone (loses/lose) when participants do not follow the rules.
     ＜解答＞ loses

582. The pack of angry wolves (howls/howl) in unison.
     ＜解答＞ howls

583. Each of the barrels (were/was) inspected carefully.
     ＜解答＞ was

584. The bundle of clothes in the first washer (is/are) mine.

    <解答> is

585. Deep sorrow and great joy (are/is) expressed in many ways.

    <解答> are

586. The number of casses of measles (has/have) decreased since last year.

    <解答> has

587. Those kinds of fruit (is/are) out of season.

    <解答> are

588. A herd of wild horses (races/race) across the plains each day.

    <解答> races

589. Not only the hills but also the lowand (makes/make) the view attractive.

    <解答> makes

590. Two village (chief/chiefs) divided the sheep among the people.

    <解答> chiefs

591. Three (deers/deer) were nibbling on the low shrub.

    <解答> deer

592. Six children worked hard to fill the two boxes with (toys/toies).

    <解答> toys

593. My two (sister-in-laws/sisters-in-law) brought armfuls of flowers.

    <解答> sisters-in-law

594. Two (manservants/menservants) stood before the Earth of Sussex.

    <解答> menservants

595. The (men's/mens') class will hold its banquet on Thursday night.

    <解答> men's

596. We laughed at the (monkies/monkeys) as they swung on the limb.

    <解答> monkeys

597. In the room, we saw three (shelfs/shelves) of old-fashioned shaving mugs.

    <解答> shelves

598. Did a team of eight (oxes/oxen) pull the heavy wagon ?

    <解答> oxen

599. He could never remember that there are two (as'/a's) in separate.

    <解答> a's

600. On the boat I met three Russians and four (Germen/Germans).

    <解答> Germans

601. Several million (dollars'/dollar's) worth of surplus farm products were shipped
    to the East.

    <解答> dollars'

602. It was (she/her), not I, who wrote the winning theme.

    <解答> she

603. All of the team except (she/her) and Betty received betters.

    <解答> her

604. Do you really think that Charles and (he/him) will come ?

    <解答> he

605. The wild horse raised (it's/its) head and stared at us for a few seconds.

    <解答> its

606. Only Father and (I/myself) went to the family reunion.

    <解答> I

607. (We/Us) boys will replace the windows that were broken by us.

    <解答> We

608. Larry promised to send Carol and (I/me) a copy of his report.

    <解答> me

609. Although Bert is taller than (I/me). I am heavier than he.

    <解答> I

610. Do you think that Romon will graduate as soon as (us/we) ?

    <解答> we

611. (Who/Whom) have you invited as guest speaker ?

    <解答> Whom

612. Any player (who/whom) they catch must pay a forfeit.

    <解答> whom

613. He is the man (that/who) is making the test flight.
    ＜解答＞ who

614. The girl (who/whom) you saw is my best friend.
    ＜解答＞ whom

615. Give the money to (whoever/whomever) calls for it.
    ＜解答＞ whomever

616. Won't you include (they/them) on the list of honor students ?
    ＜解答＞ them

617. (Whoever/Whomever) can get the job done should do it.
    ＜解答＞ Whoever

618. (Who/Whom) did you see downtown today, Jenny ?
    ＜解答＞ Whom

619. Of all the players in the group, he is the (less/least) capable.
    ＜解答＞ least

620. Of the two classes, we have the (best/better) exhibit.
    ＜解答＞ better

621. This book is more interesting than (any/any other) that he has written.
    ＜解答＞ any other

622. The women in that country work (harder/more harder) than the men.
    ＜解答＞ harder

623. Your swing is bad, but mine is (badder/worse).
    ＜解答＞ worse

624. His parents are (wealthier/more wealthy) than mine.
    ＜解答＞ wealthier

625. Howard is smaller than (anyone else/anyone) in his class.
    ＜解答＞ anyone else

626. Of all the boys, Carlos reads the (more/most) carefully.
    ＜解答＞ most

627. Which do you like (better/best) ---- golf, polo, or tennis ?
    ＜解答＞ best

628. I like both stories, but I really prefer the (shorter/shorest).

    ＜解答＞ shorter

629. This is the (worse/worst) day that we have had this winter.

    ＜解答＞ worst

630. Ned and I (sure/surely) had a wonderful summer.

    ＜解答＞ surely

631. His father is near, but his mother is (nearer/nearest).

    ＜解答＞ nearer

632. Her answer was (correct/most correct).

    ＜解答＞ correct

633. Jack is the (timidest/most timid) boy in the class.

    ＜解答＞ most timid

634. Which do you like (more/most), French or Spannish ?

    ＜解答＞ more

635. Although most of our sugar is made from cane, we get a small amount from the sugar (beet/beat).

    ＜解答＞ beet

636. The dog seemed to be hunting for a familiar (cent/scent).

    ＜解答＞ scent

637. Nothing that we could say would (altar/alter) his opinion.

    ＜解答＞ alter

638. The delighted players found this (course/coarse) to be a golfer's paradise.

    ＜解答＞ course

639. Only an educated person can understand many (principals/principles) of science.

    ＜解答＞ principles

640. Perhaps deer, as well as people, reached this land across a (strait/straight).

    ＜解答＞ strait

641. Beyond the rugged mountains the settler found rich and fertile (plains/planes).

    ＜解答＞ plains

642. Before the (capitol/capital) building stands a tall statue.

    ＜解答＞ capitol

643. People have been told that they must earn their (bred/bread) by the sweat of their brow.

    ＜解答＞ bread

644. We certainly need a pair of (oars/ores) to be carried in our sail boat.

    ＜解答＞ oars

645. His sad story (affected/effected) her very much.

    ＜解答＞ affected

646. Many years ago the people of England decided that they would be judged by their (peers/piers), not by loads and knights.

    ＜解答＞ peers

647. The (immigrants/emigrants) had to pass through customs as they disembarked.

    ＜解答＞ immigrants

648. Moses led the children of Israel (forth/fourth) into the wilderness.

    ＜解答＞ forth

649. Her accessories are always a (compliment/complement) of a particular dress.

    ＜解答＞ complement

650. Even though the law (allowed/aloud) people certain privileges, they had to respect the rights of others.

    ＜解答＞ allowed

651. When we set out to (see/sea) the day was fair, the sun was bright, and peace was over all.

    ＜解答＞ sea

652. Your brother's car is different (from/than) mine.

    ＜解答＞ from

653. I must write a theme (besides/beside) doing my homework.

    ＜解答＞ besides

654. He does not look (as/like) he used to look.

    ＜解答＞ as

655. George and Lewis were walking (in/into) the room.

<解答>　into

656. We were waiting (for/on) him.

<解答>　for

657. Did you read in the newpaper (that/where) Basilio won a prize ?

<解答>　that

658. Franklin wants to attend the opera, (while/but) Jean prefers to stay home.

<解答>　but

659. I will attend (provided/providing) Guadalupe will.

<解答>　providing

660. You may (go either/either to) now or tomorrow.

<解答>　go either

661. I'll not complete the assignment (unless/except) you complete it also.

<解答>　unless

662. (Since/Being as) you have arrived, we can plan the game.

<解答>　Since

663. Having refused to comply (with/to) the laws of the nation, the Seminoles moved farther into the swamps of Florida.

<解答>　with

664. We cannot continue our experiment (without/unless) a special appropriation is made soon.

<解答>　unless

665. No one can doubt (but what/that) you are the right person for the job.

<解答>　that

666. When we had secured the latest data (from/off) the sheets, we were able to analyze our progress.

<解答>　from

667. The voice from (inside of/within) the house sounded ghostly and frightening .

<解答>　inside of

668. Not one of her assignments was completed; (and/consequently) she failed the course.

<解答> comsequently

669. (After/Following) his farewell address, Washington went home to Mount Vernon.

<解答> After

670. The man bought the car, and (he/I) drove away.

<解答> he

671. Some people live on the river, and (you/they) farm the delta land.

<解答> they

672. The message was for Tom, and he read (it/them) aloud.

<解答> it

673. I would like (a few/a little) salt on my vegetables.

<解答> a little

674. She bought (those/that) cards last night.

<解答> those

675. There is (too much/too many) bad news on television tonight.

<解答> too much

676. This is (too many/too much) information to learn.

<解答> too much

677. Would you like (less/fewer) coffee than this ?

<解答> less

678. No one in Spanish class knew (the/a) correct answer to Mrs. Perez's question.

<解答> the

679. Scientists hope to send (the/an) expedition to Mars during the 1980s.

<解答> an

680. If your're still thirsty, I'll make (another/other) pot of coffee.

<解答> another

681. There are thirty people in the room. Twenty are from Latin America and (the other/the others) are from Japan.

<解答>　the others

682.　We looked at four cars today. The first two were far too expensive, but (the other/others) ones were reasonably priced.

<解答>　the other

683.　John, along with twenty friends, (is/are) planning a party.

<解答>　is

684.　The quality of these recordings (is/are) not very good.

<解答>　is

685.　The effects of cigarettee smoking (have/has) been proven to be extremely harmful.

<解答>　have

686.　Advertisements on television (is/are) becoming more competitive than ever before.

<解答>　are

687.　The levels of intoxication (vary/varices) from subject to subject.

<解答>　vary

688.　The picture of the soldiers (bring/brings) back many memories.

<解答>　brings

689.　If the duties of these officers (isn't/aren't) reduced, there will not be enough time to finish the project.

<解答>　aren't

690.　The use of credit cards in place of cash (have/has) increased rapidly in recent years.

<解答>　has

691.　A number of reporters (was/were) at the conference yesterday.

<解答>　were

692.　A pair of jeans (was/were) in the washing machine this morning.

<解答>　was

693.　After she had perused the materials, the secretary decided that everything (was/were) in order.

<解答> was

694. The crowd at the basketball game (was/were) wild with excitement.
<解答> was

695. The army (has/have) eliminated this section of the training test.
<解答> has

696. The number of students who have withdrawn from class this quarter (is/are) appalling.
<解答> is

697. You'll stick (your/yourself) with the pins if you are not careful.
<解答> yourself

698. Al's father doesn't approve of his (going/to go) to Europe.
<解答> going

699. We found it very difficult (reaching/to reach) a decision.
<解答> to reach

700. We are eager (to return/returning) to school in the fall.
<解答> to return

701. Mary regrets (to be/being) the one to have to tell him.
<解答> being

702. George pretended (to be/being) sick yesterday.
<解答> to be

703. Helen was anxious (to tell/telling) her family about her promotion.
<解答> telling

704. Richard is expecting (us/our) to go to class tomorrow.
<解答> us

705. You shouldn't rely on (him/his) calling you in the morning.
<解答> his

706. We object to the defense (attorney/attorney's) calling the extra witness.
<解答> attorney's

707. They are looking forward to (us/our) visiting them.
<解答> our

708. It's too hot and my hair needs (cut/cutting).

＜解答＞ cutting

709. Mary will need (to make/making) a new dress for the party.

＜解答＞ to make

710. She has already written her composition, and so (have/do) her friends.

＜解答＞ have

711. I should go grocery shopping this afternoon, and so (should/had) my neighbor.

＜解答＞ should

712. Our Spanish teacher loves to travel, and so (do/love) we.

＜解答＞ do

713. The children shouldn't take that medicine, and (neither/either) should she.

＜解答＞ neither

714. The Yankees couldn't play due to the bad weather, and (either/neither) could the Angels.

＜解答＞ neither

715. They won't have to work on weekends, and we won't (neither/either).

＜解答＞ either

716. Michael doesn't speak English, and his family doesn't (either/neither).

＜解答＞ either

717. They didn't want anything to drink, and neither (did/didn't) we.

＜解答＞ did

718. The students won't accept the dean's decession, and the faculty (won't/will) either.

＜解答＞ won't

719. Don't worry. Some day you will get used to (speaking/speak) English.

＜解答＞ speaking

720. He used to (dance/dancing) every night, but now he studies.

＜解答＞ dance

721. The policeman would rather (work/worked) on Saturday than on Sunday.

＜解答＞ work

722. Mr. Jones would rather (stayed/have stayed) home last night.

    ＜解答＞ have stayed

723. The photographer would rather that we (stood/stand) closer together than we are standing.

    ＜解答＞ stood

724. She would rather that you (not arrived/had not arrived) last night.

    ＜解答＞ had not arrived

725. Eve had to pay five dollars because she wrote a bad check. She (should/must) have deposited her money before she wrote a check.

    ＜解答＞ should

726. Alexis failed the exam. He (must/should) not have studied enough.

    ＜解答＞ must

727. George missed class today. He might (have had/had had) an accident.

    ＜解答＞ had had

728. Robert arrived without his book. He (could/would) have lost it.

    ＜解答＞ could

729. Henry's car stopped on the highway. It may (run/have run) out of gas.

    ＜解答＞ have run

730. The campers remained (calm/calmly) despite the thunderstorm.

    ＜解答＞ calm

731. Professor Calandra looked (quick/quickly) at the students' sketches.

    ＜解答＞ quickly

732. Our neighbors appeared (relaxed/relaxedly) after their vacation.

    ＜解答＞ relaxed

733. The music sounded too (noisy/noisily) to be classical.

    ＜解答＞ noisy

734. The boys felt (worse/bad) than the girls about losing the game.

    ＜解答＞ worse

735. The twins have less money at the end of the month (than/then) they have at the beginning.

<解答>　than

736. This is the (creamier/creamiest) ice cream I have had in a long time.
　　　<解答>　creamiest

737. This poster is (colorfuler/more colorful) than the one in the hall.
　　　<解答>　more colorful

738. While trying to balance the baskets on her head, the woman walked (awkwarder/more awkwardly) than her daughter.
　　　<解答>　more awkwardly

739. This painting is (less impressive/least impressive) than the one in the other gallery.
　　　<解答>　less impressive

740. Dean was (such/so) a powerful swimmer that he always won the races.
　　　<解答>　such

741. We had (such/so) wonderful memories of that place that we decided to return.
　　　<解答>　such

742. He worked (so/such) carefully that it took him a long time to complete the project.
　　　<解答>　so

743. There were (so/such) many people on the bus that we decided to walk.
　　　<解答>　so

744. The teacher made Juan (to leave/leave) the room.
　　　<解答>　leave

745. Toshiko had her car (repaired/repair) by a mechanic.
　　　<解答>　repaired

746. The policemen made the suspect (lie/lying) on the ground.
　　　<解答>　lie

747. We will have to get the Dean (to sign/sign) this form.
　　　<解答>　to sign

748. Geme got his book (publish/published) by a subsidy publisher.
　　　<解答>　published

749. Although he has been driving for fifteen years, he doesn't (know how/know) to change a tire properly.
　　＜解答＞ know how

750. The owner of the store was away, but she (knew/knew how) about the robbery.
　　＜解答＞ knew

751. (In spite of/Although) his physical handicap, he has become a successful businessman.
　　＜解答＞ In spite of

752. The child ate the cookie (even though/despite) his mother had told him not to.
　　＜解答＞ even though

753. You will see on the map that the Public Auditorium (lies/lays) north of the lake.
　　＜解答＞ lies

754. The workers were (lying/laying) cement for the patio when it began to rain.
　　＜解答＞ laying

755. The comedian always (tells/says) his friends funny jokes when he is at a party.
　　＜解答＞ tells

756. The judge instructed the witness to (tell/say) the whole truth about the accident.
　　＜解答＞ tell

757. Our teacher (said/told) that we would not have any homework during the vacation.
　　＜解答＞ said

758. Compassionate friends tried to console the (crying/cried) victims of the accident.
　　＜解答＞ crying

759. When James noticed the (burning/burnt) building, he notified the fire department immediately.
　　＜解答＞ burning

760. The (exciting/excited) passengers jumped into the lifeboats when notified that the ship was sinking.
　　＜解答＞ excited

761. Our representative presented the (approving/approved) plan to the public.

    ＜解答＞ approved

762. We found it difficult to get through the (closing/closed) door without a key.

    ＜解答＞ closed

763. The police towed away the (parking/parked) cars because they were blocking the entrance.

    ＜解答＞ parked

764. The twins have the (same/same indentical) birthmarks on their backs.

    ＜解答＞ same

765. I think we have (sufficient enough/enough) information to write the report.

    ＜解答＞ enough

766. When the roads became too slippery, we decided to (return back/return) to the cabin and wait for the storm to subside.

    ＜解答＞ return

767. The mountain climbers (proceeded forward/proceeded) on their long trek up the side of the mountain.

    ＜解答＞ proceeded

768. I think that we should come up with a (new/new innovation) for doing this job.

    ＜解答＞ new

769. My cousins love to play with the (two/two twins) from across the street.

    ＜解答＞ two

770. The puppy stood up slowly, wagged its tail, (blinked/blinking) its eyes, and barked.

    ＜解答＞ blinked

771. The chief of police demanded from his assistants an orderly investigation, a well-written report, and (that they work hard/hard work).

    ＜解答＞ hard work

772. The farmer plows the fields, plants the seeds, and (will harvest/harvests) the crop.

    ＜解答＞ harvests

773. Abraham Lincoln was a good president ---- self educated, hard working, and (always told the truth/honest).

    ＜解答＞ honest

774. Children love playing in the mud, running through puddles, and (they get very dirty/getting very dirty).

    ＜解答＞ getting very dirty

775. Despite America's affluence, many people are without jobs, on welfare, and (have a lot of debts/in debt).

    ＜解答＞ in debt

776. The recuers were a welcome (cite/sight) for those trapped on the snow-covered mountain.

    ＜解答＞ sight

777. (Who's/Whose) supposed to supply the refreshments for tonight's meeting ?

    ＜解答＞ Who's

778. It is a (costume/custom) in the United States to eat turky on Thanksgiving.

    ＜解答＞ custom

779. Although my mother never eats (desert/dessert), I prefer something sweet.

    ＜解答＞ dessert

780. I guess (their/they're) not interested because we have not heard from them.

    ＜解答＞ they're

781. Nobody had any (stationary/stationery) so we had to use notebook paper to write the letter.

    ＜解答＞ stationery

782. Doris and Marge teach kindergarten; the (latter/later) works in Putnam.

    ＜解答＞ latter

783. Lisa had to (quit/quite) eating apples after the orthodontist put braces on her teeth.

    ＜解答＞ quit

784. After declaring bankruptcy, the company was forced to (liquely / liquidate) its assets.

　　＜解答＞ liquidate

785. Keith's company's headquarters were (formerly/formally) located in Philadelphin.

　　＜解答＞ formerly

786. (Especially/Special) attention must be given to the questions at the end of each chapter.

　　＜解答＞ Special

787. By asking many questions, the instruction tried to (elicit/illicit) information from the students.

　　＜解答＞ elicit

788. A large (number/quantity) of whales beached and died last year because of ear problems.

　　＜解答＞ number

789. When Louise set the table, she placed the silverware (besides/beside) the plates.

　　＜解答＞ beside

790. Mark is (sensible/sensitive) enough to swim close to shore.

　　＜解答＞ sensible

791. The government will (perseute/prosecute) the guilty for polluting the waters.

　　＜解答＞ prosecute

792. Dante's (immoral/immortal) literary masterpieces are read in universities across the country.

　　＜解答＞ immortal

793. Eric's courageous rescue of the drowning child was a (credulous/creditable) deed.

　　＜解答＞ creditable

794. Perry's spare flashlight was (helpless/useless) the night of the storm because the batteries were corroded.

　　＜解答＞ useless

795. The gaudy decorations in the hall (detracted/distracted) from the beauty of the celebration.

    <解答> detracted

796. There are trees (on/in) both sides of the highway.

    <解答> on

797. He concentrated all his energy (on/in) doing his work.

    <解答> on

798. She saw (in/on) the boy the very image of his father at that age.

    <解答> in

799. The students were leaving school (in/on) twos and threes.

    <解答> in

800. He wrote the letter in pencil instead of (with/by) the ink.

    <解答> with

801. (At/By) the time I return from America next year, he will have graduated from college.

    <解答> By

802. He informed me of the news (by/with) letter not by telephone.

    <解答> by

803. He stopped going to school (for/on) the time being.

    <解答> for

804. Much (to/for) my disappointment, he had brought no toys for me.

    <解答> to

805. (From/Of) a practical point of view, his experiment was a splendid success.

    <解答> From

806. He succeeded in his work (with/to) the help of his friends.

    <解答> with

807. He was elected by a majority of 30 votes (to/against) 20.

    <解答> against

808. We (aren't/don't) watching a television program now.

    <解答> aren't

809. Mr. Johnson (doesn't/aren't) always eat at that place.

    ＜解答＞ doesn't

810. Mr. Moore (teaches/is teaching) English from 2:00 to 4:p.m.

    ＜解答＞ teaches

811. Alice and Mary (put away/are putting away) the dinner dishes right now.

    ＜解答＞ are putting away

812. Frank (borrows/borrowed) some money from his friend last night.

    ＜解答＞ borrowed

813. Did the man (read/rode) the instructions in the book very carefully.

    ＜解答＞ read

814. The students didn't (brought/bring) their distionaries to class yesterday.

    ＜解答＞ bring

815. (Is/Are) Smith and Creen collecting information for Mr. Johnson.

    ＜解答＞ Are

816. I didn't have (any/some) trouble with my homework last night.

    ＜解答＞ any

817. The children are eating (some/any) ice cream in the kitchen.

    ＜解答＞ some

818. (No one/Anyone) finished the examination before three o'clock.

    ＜解答＞ No one

819. The chairman didn't get suggestions from (anyone/no one) in the audience.

    ＜解答＞ anyone

820. Will you be ready before three o'clock ? No, I (won't/am not).

    ＜解答＞ won't

821. Is there going to be a meeting tonight ? Yes, (there is/it is).

    ＜解答＞ there is

822. Does the bus stop at the next corner ? Yes, (it is/it does).

    ＜解答＞ it does

823. Did the woman attend the meeting too ? No, (she didn't/she wasn't).

    ＜解答＞ she didn't

824. The two girls (do already/have already done) the dinner dishes.

<解答> have already done

825. Mr. Berg has studied English in this class (for/since) eight months.

<解答> for

826. Alice has been here (since/for) the beginning of the year.

<解答> since

827. Frank's parents have lived in their new apartment (since/in) last fall.

<解答> since

828. Mr. Johnson had several important meetings (in/since) the morning.

<解答> in

829. My wife and I usually tak our vacation (in/for) the summer.

<解答> in

830. Fred's sister has her diploma (for/in) over six weeks now.

<解答> for

831. Alice has been absent (from/to) the last two classes.

<解答> from

832. Everyone feels very sorry (for/of) that poor old man.

<解答> for

833. That kind of dress is not suitable (for/about) certain occasions.

<解答> for

834. The quality of this shirt is not equal (to/at) the quality of that one.

<解答> to

835. Why were those girls mad (at/to) Frank and you ?

<解答> at

836. Are you fellows (still/any more) worrying about the same problem ?

<解答> still

837. Richard and I don't eat lunch at the cafeteria (any more/still).

<解答> any more

838. Most of the students have done those two lessons (already/yet).

<解答> already

839. Not many people in this neighborhood have heard the news (yet/already).
＜解答＞ yet

840. The Browns have (yet/already) had their new car for two weeks.
＜解答＞ already

841. Have you seen the movie at the Paramount Theater (already/yet) ?
＜解答＞ yet

842. Frank collects stamps. He (also/too) collects interesting coins.
＜解答＞ also

843. They (always/usually) have tried to follow his instruction very carefully.
＜解答＞ always

844. Why doesn't that student (ever/never) write his lessons carefully ?
＜解答＞ ever

845. That store (seldom/ever) receives complaints from its customers.
＜解答＞ seldom

846. Mr. Fox (never/ever) smokes cigars in the office during the day.
＜解答＞ never

847. The director of our office is a (good/well) educated man.
＜解答＞ well

848. His knowledge of English grammar is quite (well/good).
＜解答＞ well

849. We are using this room for our English class (temporary/temporaryly).
＜解答＞ temporaryly

850. Have the students finished their compositions or (no/not) ?
＜解答＞ not

851. (Not/No) much time remains before the final examination.
＜解答＞ Not

852. (No/Not) students were invited to the committee meeting.
＜解答＞ No

853. I had (much/many) more trouble with this lesson than the last one.
＜解答＞ much

854. Football is (much/many) more popular than soccer in this country.
    <解答> much

855. There are (many/much) more tall buildings in New York than in Paris.
    <解答> many

856. The design of that house is similar (to/from) the design of this one.
    <解答> to

857. Your example was quite different (as/from) the one in the book.
    <解答> from

858. His answer to the problem wasn't quite the same (as/to) mine.
    <解答> as

859. His explanation of the lesson was (clear/clearer) than yours.
    <解答> clearer

860. In general, Marjorie does (more careful/careful) work than I do.
    <解答> more careful

861. (The most/The more) beautiful house in the whole neighborhood is that one.
    <解答> The most

862. You look much (the happiest/happier) today than you did yesterday.
    <解答> happier

863. English (taught/is taught) in the schools of almost every nation.
    <解答> is taught

864. The noise from the trains (annoyed/was annoyed) me terribly last night.
    <解答> annoyed

865. Not much (had said/has been said) about the matter since that time.
    <解答> has been said

866. All the students (brought/will bring) guests to the party tomorrow night.
    <解答> will bring

867. Less than half of the cans of paint (used/have been used) up to now.
    <解答> have been used

868. Frank (should not tell/should tell not) anyone about his plans until next summer.

<解答> should not tell

869. Mr. Foster ought not to (write/have written) to them about that matter last week.

    <解答> have written

870. All members of the club must (to pay/pay) their dues before Friday.

    <解答> pay

871. The men didn't (have to/had to) show some kind of identification.

    <解答> have to

872. You must (not help/don't help) your two friends with their homework.

    <解答> not help

873. Students (should/ought) spend much time on their homework.

    <解答> should

874. Bill (can/will be able) help us with the work next week.

    <解答> can

875. She (couldn't/wasn't able) to find her silver bracelet.

    <解答> wasn't able

876. We (can't/won't be able) to visit you next weekend.

    <解答> won't be able

877. It was very uncomfortable (to sit/sitting) in one place for so long.

    <解答> to sit

878. (Getting/To get) to school by bus usually takes me forty minutes.

    <解答> Getting

879. We have never forgiven him (for making/to make) that sarcastic remark.

    <解答> for making

880. The witness was very anxious (about testifying/to testify) in a courtroom.

    <解答> about testifying

881. Are you accustomed (to hear/to hearing) those airplanes over your house ?

    <解答> to hearing

882. Have you ever considered (to try/trying) something different ?

    <解答> trying

883. Those men deny (knowing/to know) anything at all about it.
　　　＜解答＞　knowing

884. I hesitate (to say/saying) anything to him about the mistake.
　　　＜解答＞　to say

885. The fellow really resents (taking/to take) orders from other people.
　　　＜解答＞　taking

886. Are you going to suggest (to travel/traveling) by train or not ?
　　　＜解答＞　traveling

887. It is impossible (to do/doing) that without any help from you.
　　　＜解答＞　to do

888. We would appreciate (being informed/to be informed) about the matter promptly.
　　　＜解答＞　being informed

889. Naturally, I would like (to be promoted/being promoted) to a higher position.
　　　＜解答＞　to be promoted

890. My brother won't be at home tomorrow night, but I (will/won't).
　　　＜解答＞will

891. The other students didn't enjoy the trip yesterday, but I (did/didn't).
　　　＜解答＞　did

892. Mary Peters comes to work on time, but no one else (does/doesn't).
　　　＜解答＞　does

893. I finished my work on time, but none of the other students (do/don't).
　　　＜解答＞　do

894. No one else did that work, and I don't intend (to/to do that work) either.
　　　＜解答＞　to

895. I haven't spoken to my boss yet, but I (ought to/ought to speak to him) very soon.
　　　＜解答＞　ought to

896. The (running/run) water flowed over the edge of the sink.
　　　＜解答＞　running

897. Many famous authors write book under (assuming/assumed) names.
    <解答> assumed

898. They have already decided (which one/one) they're going to buy.
    <解答> which one

899. The doctor I (went to/went) last week specializes in surgery.
    <解答> went to

900. Mr. Thompson thought we (should/shall) go to the meeting tomorrow.
    <解答> should

901. Miss Adams said she (must/had to) leave early tomorrow morning.
    <解答> had to

902. We assumed that the meeting (will/would) be over by that time.
    <解答> would

903. We assume that the man (can/could) help us with the work.
    <解答> can

904. Our friends asked us why we (came/had come) there so early.
    <解答> had come

905. He thought we (should send/should have sent) the wire next week.
    <解答> should send

906. It is strange that fellow (doesn't/didn't) try to find a good job.
    <解答> doesn't

907. I was delighted the guests (had had/have had) a good time up to them.
    <解答> had had

908. We were happy Charles (can/could) come with us after all.
    <解答> could

909. I couldn't imagine what (had he/he had) found.
    <解答> he had

910. He didn't know whose book (that was/was that).
    <解答> that was

911. He (said/told) that he had enjoyed the trip to France a great deal.
    <解答> said

912. My friend (told/said) me that he was planning to leave right away.
    ＜解答＞ told

913. I will recommend that student (speaks/speak) to the director.
    ＜解答＞ speak

914. Our boss insisted that we (were/be) careful with that machine.
    ＜解答＞ be

915. Carl left for home early (because/because of) he had to study.
    ＜解答＞ because

916. I sent the letter airmail so that he (will/would) get it right away.
    ＜解答＞ would

917. The man spoke (so/such) rapidly that I couldn't understand him.
    ＜解答＞ so

918. Ralph bought that used car (although/because) we advised him against it.
    ＜解答＞ although

919. The weather is better today (than/than it was) yesterday.
    ＜解答＞ than it was

920. Would you please put the book where (it belongs/belongs).
    ＜解答＞ it belongs

921. (Where/Wherever) we went, we seemed to see very interesting things.
    ＜解答＞ Wherever

922. (What/When) I visited Rome, I saw the famous coliseum.
    ＜解答＞ When

923. (Before/After) the secretary leaves, she will put the letters on your desk.
    ＜解答＞ Before

924. If I had had enough time, I (would/will) have gone to the meeting with you.
    ＜解答＞ would

925. (For/Since) Mr. Fox was sick, he had to cancel the appointment.
    ＜解答＞ Since

926. I couldn't hear the speaker, (so/so that) I moved to the first row.
    ＜解答＞ so that

927. I had such a wonderful time (as/that) I didn't want to go home.
＜解答＞ that

928. Although he's 65 years old, (but Mr. Cole/Mr. Cole) is still an active man.
＜解答＞ Mr. Cole

929. There are as many students in this class (as there are/as) in that one.
＜解答＞ as there are

930. Our dog Saki usually goes (when/wherever) he wishes to go.
＜解答＞ wherever

931. The Browns saw the Eiffel Tower (that/when) they were in Paris.
＜解答＞ when

932. George and I will wait right here (during/until) you get back.
＜解答＞ until

933. I will give Mr. Anderson your message (if/whether) I see him tomorrow.
＜解答＞ if

934. (Since/Because) Don often forgets things, his wife usually gives him a list.
＜解答＞ Since

935. I borrowed ten dollars from Ed (because/so that) I could pay for my books.
＜解答＞ so that

936. I borrow the money from him (because/so that) I had to pay for my books.
＜解答＞ because

937. (Although/Despite) he is not well, educated, that man has a good position.
＜解答＞Although

938. (Despite/Although) the narrow streets in that city, many people drive cars.
＜解答＞ Despite

939. That student speaks fluently (in spite of/because of) his limited vacabulary.
＜解答＞ in spite of

940. Bill (was having/had) breakfast when I stopped at his home this morning.
＜解答＞ was having

941. When I left my office last night, it (was still raining/still rained) very hard.
＜解答＞ was still raining

942. When the students (were hearing/heard) the bell, they got up and left.

　　＜解答＞ heard

943. When I (saw/was seeing) the fire truck, I put on my brakes immediately.

　　＜解答＞ saw

944. When I (was hearing/heard) the loud crash cutside, I ran to the window.

　　＜解答＞ heard

945. The manager (had just closed/just closed) the store a moment before I got there.

　　＜解答＞ had just closed

946. The man wouldn't leave until he (had received/received) a definite answer.

　　＜解答＞ had received

947. When we (get/got) the photographs, we'll show them to you.

　　＜解答＞ get

948. You should ask the boss about it before you (made/make) any changes.

　　＜解答＞ make

949. I (speak/will speak) to you about that matter after the meeting tonight.

　　＜解答＞ will speak

950. I (help/will help) you with your homework as soon as I finish this letter.

　　＜解答＞ will help

951. Mr. Brink (will be crossing/crosses) the Atlantic by the time the news reaches him.

　　＜解答＞ will be crossing

952. When you go into the office, Mrs. Roland (is sitting/will be sitting) at the front desk.

　　＜解答＞ will be sitting

953. Jack says he (will be returning/will return) the money to you at two o'clock tomorrow.

　　＜解答＞ will return

954. You will have enough time to eat lunch if you (get/had got) here early.

　　＜解答＞ get

955. If I (decide/decided) to join the club, I will fill out this application blank.

＜解答＞ decide

956. Father will surely get wet today if he (not takes/not took) his umbrella.

＜解答＞ not takes

957. If you (were not/are not) more careful in the future, you'll have an accident.

＜解答＞ are not

958. If anyone (asked/asks) for you, I will tell him to call back later today.

＜解答＞ asks

959. If I (am/were) the mayor of this city, I would change certain things.

＜解答＞ were

960. I would gladly tell the answer if I only (know/knew) it myself.

＜解答＞ knew

961. If the weather (was/were) better right now, we could go for a walk.

＜解答＞ were

962. If the weather (was/had been) better, we would have left Friday morning.

＜解答＞ had been

963. I could have lent you some money if I (hadn't spent/wouldn't spend) everything.

＜解答＞ hadn't spent

964. We would have bought that house if the price (had been/will be) a little lower.

＜解答＞ had been

965. (If/Unless) you don't study harder, you're going to fail the examination.

＜解答＞ If

966. (Unless/If) you invest your money wisely, you will lose all of it.

＜解答＞ Unless

967. (If no/Unless no) more guests come, there will be enough food for everyone.

＜解答＞ If no

968. Our dog wouldn't have barked (if/unless) he hadn't heard a strange noise.

＜解答＞if

969. I wish it (were/had been) possible for me to help you with it yesterday.
    ＜解答＞ had been

970. I wish someone (would offer/will offer) to help me with that work tomorrow.
    ＜解答＞ would offer

971. I wish I (have/had) more time now to help you with your lesson.
    ＜解答＞ had

972. I didn't use to (enjoy/enjoying) classical music, but I listen to it regularly now.
    ＜解答＞ enjoying

973. Mr. Moore is used to (hear/hearing) many different accents.
    ＜解答＞ hearing

974. We are accustomed to (bearing/bear) the noise of the airplane's now.
    ＜解答＞ bearing

975. We soon became accustomed to (write/writing) everything in English.
    ＜解答＞ writing

976. You'll get used to (play/playing) your new piano very soon.
    ＜解答＞ playing

977. The work was supposed to (be finished/being finished) yesterday afternoon.
    ＜解答＞ be finished

978. The plane from Miami is supposed to (get/getting) here ten minutes from now.
    ＜解答＞ get

979. The committee (should approve/could approve) the plan at the meeting tomorrow.
    ＜解答＞ should approve

980. We (should have received/should receive) a telegram from Mr. Cole last night.
    ＜解答＞ should have received

981. I (must/ought) go to the bank right away in order to cash this check.
    ＜解答＞ must

982. You (thought/must think) I don't have a job because I'm at home so often.
    ＜解答＞ must think

983. George (must assume/must have assumed) that we had already taken care of the matter.

　　＜解答＞ must have assumed

984. (Hadn't/Haven't) we better tell them that we won't be able to meet them ?

　　＜解答＞ Hadn't

985. You'd better not (say/to say) anything to Mr. Wilson about the matter.

　　＜解答＞ say

986. You shouldn't (leave/to leave) the building until you get permission.

　　＜解答＞ leave

987. I really (would/should) enjoying having a chance to meet all of your friends.

　　＜解答＞ would

988. I (will/would) prefer seeing a movie to watching television tonight.

　　＜解答＞ would

989. I (shall/would) like to eat dinner earlier than usual tonight.

　　＜解答＞ would

990. (Wouldn't/Hadn't) you rather walk downtown this afternoon ?

　　＜解答＞ Wouldn't

991. I (would/had) rather meet you in the lobby of the building than on the corner.

　　＜解答＞ would

992. I wrote the lesson last night and handed (it in/in it) this morning.

　　＜解答＞ it in

993. If you go to the second counter, the clerk there will wait (on you/you on).

　　＜解答＞ on you

994. If you keep on wearing that suit every day, you'll wear (it out/out it).

　　＜解答＞ it out

995. We like to get away (from/off) the city during the hot summer months.

　　＜解答＞ from

996. Are you anxious to get back (to/on) work after your vacation ?

　　＜解答＞ to

997. It's impossible to do away (with/from) classroom discipline completely.

<解答>　with

998. That building is taller than (any other/the other) in the city of New York.

<解答>　any other

999. I really can't go now, I'll have to go with you (some other/other) day.

<解答>　some other

1000. They (accept/except) my invitation to dinner.

<解答>　accept

1001. A student has much less liberty there than in (other/another) countries.

<解答>　other

1002. Everyone attended the meeting (accept/except) the secretary.

<解答>　except

1003. The movie had (already/all ready) begun by the time we arrived.

<解答>　already

1004. He checked out a large (amount/number) of books from the library.

<解答>　number

1005. Elephants can consume a large (number/amount) of food.

<解答>　amount

1006. The mail arrived (around/about) ten o'clock.

<解答>　about

1007. She had a coat (about/around) her shoulders.

<解答>　around

1008. I (couldn't/could) hardly see him in the dark.

<解答>　could

1009. She (didn't earn/earned) but thirty dollars last week.

<解答>　earned

1010. He (doesn't spend/spends) scarcely any money on clothes.

<解答>　spends

1011. They (did/made) a peaceful agreement.

<解答>　made

1012. I never (make/do) fun of other people.

　　＜解答＞ make

1013. It's time to (do/make) the sandwiches.

　　＜解答＞ make

1014. Rarely does he (make/do) a mistake.

　　＜解答＞ make

1015. I'll (do/make) the arrangements for party.

　　＜解答＞ make

1016. Before she left the house, she (made/did) her bed.

　　＜解答＞ made

1017. The president (made/did) an interesting speach, didn't he ?

　　＜解答＞ made

1018. My father refuses to (make/do) business with dishonest people.

　　＜解答＞ do

1019. The teacher (made/did) the examination difficult.

　　＜解答＞ made

1020. Will you (make/do) me a small favor ?

　　＜解答＞ do

1021. He (thinks/expects) to graduate in May.

　　＜解答＞ expects

1022. He (supposes/expects) that he will marry next year.

　　＜解答＞ supposes

1023. He (thinks/expects) that he will go to the Unites States next summer.

　　＜解答＞ thinks

1024. I (think/expect) that he is busy now.

　　＜解答＞ think

1025. I (suppose/expect) to see you tomorrow.

　　＜解答＞ expect

1026. He was so tired that he stopped playing for (few/a few) minutes.

　　＜解答＞ a few

1027. There were (a few/few) chairs left, so that I had to stand up.

＜解答＞ few

1028. The meeting was canceled because (few/a few) members attended.

＜解答＞few

1029. You had better (to pay/pay) attention to the details.

＜解答＞ pay

1030. Which movie would you rather (to see/see) ?

＜解答＞ see

1031. She says that she would rather not (have/to have) dessert.

＜解答＞ have

1032. You should avoid making (these/this) kinds of mistakes.

＜解答＞ these

1033. Those (sort/sorts) of insects are harmful to man.

＜解答＞ sorts

1034. Men of his (type/types) are not to be trusted.

＜解答＞ type

1035. What (kind of a/kind of) telephone did the company install ?

＜解答＞ kind of

1036. The vicuma is a shy (type of an/type of) animal.

＜解答＞ type of

1037. Jefferson and Lincoln are two famous presidents. The (latter/later) was assassinated while in office.

＜解答＞ latter

1038. We must all die sooner or (later/latter).

＜解答＞ later

1039. Would you mind (loaning/lending) me your pencil ?

＜解答＞ lending

1040. I needed money, so John (lent/loaned) me some.

＜解答＞ lent

1041. She doesn't study (as/like) she should.

   <解答> as

1042. You ought to write (like/as) me.

   <解答> like

1043. (As/Like) the coach said, the team performed well.

   <解答> As

1044. She acts (as if/like) she doesn't understand.

   <解答> as if

1045. He spoke (as though/like) he understood what he was talking about.

   <解答> as though

1046. (May be/Maybe) the sun will come out tomorrow.

   <解答> Maybe

1047. The secretary (may be/maybe) out to lunch.

   <解答> may be

1048. When I asked, she (past/passed) me the sugar.

   <解答> passed

1049. I (passed/past) his house on the way to the post office.

   <解答> passed

1050. In (passed/past) times, salt was often used as money.

   <解答> past

1051. One can learn from experiences in his (passed/past).

   <解答> past

1052. Many students prefer history (to/than) mathematics.

   <解答> to

1053. I believe that a microwave oven is superior (than/to) a conventional oven.

   <解答> to

1054. The reason he makes poor grades is (that/because) he never studies.

   <解答> that

1055. My reason for using a typewriter is (because/that) my handwriting is poor.

   <解答> that

1056. Students find that mathematical concept (some/somewhat) difficult.

　　＜解答＞ somewhat

1057. His shirt looks (somewhat/some) dirty.

　　＜解答＞ somewhat

1058. You should try (and/to) write legibly.

　　＜解答＞ to

1059. I am going to try (to/and) get some sleep tonight.

　　＜解答＞ to

1060. Be sure (and/to) bring a pencil to class tomorrow.

　　＜解答＞ to

1061. My nucle has trouble breathing; he isn't (supposed/suppose) to smoke.

　　＜解答＞ supposed

1062. I (used/use) to enjoying gardening.

　　＜解答＞ used

1063. My friend was late, I had to (wait on/wait for) him for half an hour.

　　＜解答＞ wait for

1064. Good clerks are happy to (wait on/wait for) their customers.

　　＜解答＞ wait on

1065. I read in the newspaper (where/that) crime is on the increase.

　　＜解答＞ that

1066. Have you noticed (where/that) people are smoking less than they used to ?

　　＜解答＞ that

1067. (Although/While) my family is not rich, we have many advantages.

　　＜解答＞ Although

1068. (While/Although) I was not busy, I couldn't help him.

　　＜解答＞ Although

1069. I was (adviced/advised) to purchase an economical car.

　　＜解答＞ advised

1070. His (advise/advice) was very useful.

　　＜解答＞ advice

1071. (Almost m/Most) everyone had a desire to succeed.

<解答> Almost

1072. The student was (most/almost) finished when the bell rang.

<解答> almost

1073. The children ate (most/almost) of the pie.

<解答> most

1074. (Altogether/All together) confused, he asked me to explain the work again.

<解答> Altogether

1075. The passengers stood (altogether/all together) in the station.

<解答> all together

1076. We can talk (anywhere/anywheres).

<解答> anywhere

1077. I lost my umbrella (somewheres/somewhere) in the store.

<解答> somewhere

1078. The second and the third lessons were (equally as/equally) difficult.

<解答> equally

1079. Jim is (as equally tall/as tall as) his brother-in-law.

<解答> as tall as

1080. He spends (less/fewer) time on his studies than on his golf game.

<解答> less

1081. I am writing (in regards to/in regard to) your letter of May 10.

<解答> in regard to

1082. (As regards/In regards to) money, I have enough.

<解答> As regards

1083. Now, (in regards to/regarding) money, what is to be done ?

<解答> regarding

1084. The human body and (it's/its) organs are interesting to study.

<解答> its

1085. I always (lie/lay) down after I eat dinner.

<解答> lie

1086. He (laid/lay) down because he had a headache.
　　＜解答＞ lay

1087. The books are (lying/laying) on the table.
　　＜解答＞ lying

1088. The teacher (lay/laid) her books on the table when she entered the room.
　　＜解答＞ laid

1089. The boys have (laid/lain) under the trees for hours.
　　＜解答＞ lain

1090. This machine is easy to operate; you need (a little/little) skill.
　　＜解答＞ little

1091. He has had difficulty in finding a job because he has (little/a little) education.
　　＜解答＞ little

1092. She will (lose/loose) weight if she goes on a diet.
　　＜解答＞ lose

1093. One of the knobs on the drawer is (lose/loose).
　　＜解答＞ loose

1094. Only Bill and (I/myself) witnessed the accident.
　　＜解答＞ I

1095. The tires of the car are bad, but (itself/the car itself) is in good condition.
　　＜解答＞ the car itself

1096. They did the work by (themselves/theirselves).
　　＜解答＞ themselves

1097. The little boy was extremely intelligent, he taught (him/himself) to read.
　　＜解答＞ himself

1098. Tigers (seldom if ever/seldom ever) eat human beings.
　　＜解答＞ seldom if ever

1099. I (hardly ever/seldom or ever) see him nowadays.
　　＜解答＞ hardly ever

1100. Taxes are (so/very) high today that some people try to cheat on their tax returns.

<解答> so

1101. Professor Davis is (such/so) a good lecturer that students enjoy being in his class.

<解答> such

1102. I will do the (very/so) best I can.

<解答> very

1103. John is (too clever/clever enough) to solve the problem.

<解答> clever enough

1104. The weather is (too/very) cold to go swimming.

<解答> too

1105. The actor is (very/too) nervous to go on stage.

<解答> too

1106. My father wants (me to do/that I do) well in school.

<解答> me to do

1107. She wants (to pass/that she can pass) the test.

<解答> to pass

1108. The person with (whom/which) I had the argument was the chairman.

<解答> whom

1109. (Who/Whom) did you speak to about your problem.

<解答> whom

1110. (Who/Whom) did you say ruled the country at that time ?

<解答> Who

1111. John Kennedy was a man (whom/who) many people admired.

<解答> whom

1112. (Would/Will) you like a cup of coffee now ?

<解答> Would

1113. I have never met your parents, but I (would/will) like to know them.

<解答> would

1114. My boss told me that he (would/will) increase my salary next year.

<解答> would

1115. We heard on the radio that it (will/would) rain tomorrow.
   ＜解答＞ would

1116. The physician appeared (nervous/nervously) when he talked to the patient.
   ＜解答＞ nervously

1117. We all agreed that the new film was (really/real) good.
   ＜解答＞ really

1118. The students found the physics examination (extremely/extreme) difficult.
   ＜解答＞ extremely

1119. If you speak (firm/firmly), he will listen to you.
   ＜解答＞ firmly

1120. He made (considerable/considerably) more progress than I.
   ＜解答＞ considerably

1121. The professor presented an (obviously/obvious) important point in class.
   ＜解答＞ obviously

1122. It rained (steadily/steady) all day yesterday.
   ＜解答＞ steadily

1123. The dog remained (faithful/faithfully) to its master until the end.
   ＜解答＞ faithful

1124. He can do the job (easier/more easily) than you can.
   ＜解答＞ more easily

1125. The problem seemed (exceeding/exceedingly) complex to me.
   ＜解答＞ exceedingly

1126. He rarely eats at that resturant, (does/doesn't) he ?
   ＜解答＞ does

1127. I (had/hadn't) hardly gotten out the door when the phone rang again.
   ＜解答＞ had

1128. Several people arrived too (lately/late) to be admitted to the performance.
   ＜解答＞ late

1129. The horse ran (fastly/fast) enough to win the race.
   ＜解答＞ fast

1130. The architect worked (hard/hardly) to finish his drawings by the next day.

　　＜解答＞ hard

1131. Unless Terry (passes/will pass) his chemistry course, he won't graduate this semester.

　　＜解答＞ passes

1132. (Although/Because) it was raining, Anita Yefused to take her swimming lesson.

　　＜解答＞ Because

1133. Vincent will wait on the corner until the bus (will come/comes).

　　＜解答＞ comes

1134. We will continue the game after the rain (stops/will stop).

　　＜解答＞ stops

1135. He carefully taped the chemistry lecture so that he (can/could) listen to it again.

　　＜解答＞ could

1136. As soon as he (will get/gets) his check, he can buy the books he needs.

　　＜解答＞ gets

1137. Police officers stop citizens when they (drive/will drive) too fast.

　　＜解答＞ drive

1138. Before you go to bed, (you will turn off/turn off) the lights.

　　＜解答＞ turn off

1139. If anyone (has/will have) a question, I'll be happy to answer it.

　　＜解答＞ has

1140. Neither of the two women wants (her/their) office renovated.

　　＜解答＞ her

1141. I always give each of my students the attention (he/they) needs.

　　＜解答＞ he

1142. He is one of those speakers who make (their/his) ideas perfectly clear.

　　＜解答＞ their

1143. No one would wish to lose all of (his/their) money in the stock market.

　　＜解答＞ his

1144. Neither the members of the committee nor the chairman submitted (their/his) reports on time.

<解答> his

1145. My insurance company has recently increased (its/their) premiums on liability policies.

<解答> its

1146. One can find a great deal of information on world religions if (they go/he goes) to the library.

<解答> he goes

1147. A parent should never allow (themselves/himself) to neglect his children.

<解答> himself

1148. The state of Texas has changed (its/their) laws on a adoption.

<解答> its

1149. If anyone has a question, I'll see (him/them) after class.

<解答> him

1150. Which student forgot to sign (his/their) name in the proper place ?

<解答> his

1151. A lawyer must deal honestly with his clients if (he/they) wishes to maintain a good reputation.

<解答> he

1152. Many people enjoy reading about the Netherlands and (its/their) people.

<解答> its

1153. Any senior can rent (his/their) cap and gown for graduation from the bookstore.

<解答> his

1154. John and (I/me) took the last two seats.

<解答> I

1155. Janet is much more charming than (him/he).

<解答> he

1156. (Whom/who) do you believe is to blame ?

    ＜解答＞ who

1157. You may invite (whomever/whoever) you choose.

    ＜解答＞ whomever

1158. It was (them/they) who participated in the strike.

    ＜解答＞ they

1159. I gave the keys to them --- Susan and (she/her).

    ＜解答＞ her

1160. People like him and (she/her) should be punished.

    ＜解答＞ her

1161. Everyone but Don and (he/him) accepted the player's excuse for being late.

    ＜解答＞ him

1162. Between you and (I/me), the new proposal seems to be poorly written.

    ＜解答＞ me

1163. Carole, unlike (they/them), understood the mathematical equation.

    ＜解答＞ them

1164. The chairman refused to acknowledge either John or (I/me).

    ＜解答＞ me

1165. Be sure to speak to my husband or (me/I) about your suggestion.

    ＜解答＞ me

1166. (Us/We) teachers are accustomed to spending hours preparing classes.

    ＜解答＞ We

1167. The children were tired, (so that their/their) mother put them to bed.

    ＜解答＞ so that their

1168. The spider is an insect (which/it) spins a web.

    ＜解答＞ which

1169. Greenland is a large island, (but few/few) people live there.

    ＜解答＞ but few

1170. Although Greenland is a large island, (but few/few) people live there.

    ＜解答＞ few

1171. Greenland is a large island; (however/otherwise), few people live there.

　　　＜解答＞　however

1172. The Vikings ate fish (and/and they) drank ale.

　　　＜解答＞　and

1173. George Washington Carver was a slave (who/he) became a famous man.

　　　＜解答＞　who

1174. Vesuvius is a famous volcano (it/which) is located near Naples, Italy.

　　　＜解答＞　which

1175. People avoid snakes (because/because of) them are poisonous.

　　　＜解答＞　because

1176. John Kennedy is a will-known person (who/he) established the Peace Corps.

　　　＜解答＞　who

1177. That boy speaks German fluently, (he/and he) knows English too.

　　　＜解答＞　and he

1178. That boy not only speaks German fluently (but also/he) knows English.

　　　＜解答＞　but also

1179. The Thai student speaks English as (fluent/fluently) as the Frenchman.

　　　＜解答＞　fluently

1180. My information is better (than/that) theirs.

　　　＜解答＞　than

1181. She looks a great deal taller (as/than) he.

　　　＜解答＞　than

1182. I ran much (farther/further) than the other contestants.

　　　＜解答＞　further

1183. I hope that you drive more (carefuler/carefully) than he does.

　　　＜解答＞　carefully

1184. Was my composition the (most longest/longest) that you read ?

　　　＜解答＞　longest

1185. He made (as few/few) mistakes as I.

　　　＜解答＞　as few

1186. He usually does as (less/little) work as he can.

   ＜解答＞ little

1187. I looked at the two games and then chose the (easier/easiest) one.

   ＜解答＞ easier

1188. Soccer is more popular than (any/any other) sport on our campus.

   ＜解答＞ any other

1189. Calculus 102 is harder than (any other/any) course in the mathematics

   department.

   ＜解答＞ any other

1190. Are Kennedy's children more famous than (Nixon/Nixon's) ?

   ＜解答＞ Nixon's

1191. I like animals more than most (adults/adults do).

   ＜解答＞ adults do

1192. I like animals more than (I do/do) most adults.

   ＜解答＞ do

1193. If you study hard, you (pass/ will pass) the next test.

   ＜解答＞ will pass

1194. If I (lived/had lived) during the seventeenth century, I could have known Sir

   Isaac Newton.

   ＜解答＞ had lived

1195. If my friends (had/would have) a car, they would certainly pick me up.

   ＜解答＞ had

1196. If you (need/will need) help, I'll be happy to help you.

   ＜解答＞ need

1197. If you (had/would have) called, I would have gone out with you.

   ＜解答＞ had

1198. The dog will bite you if you (will enter/enter) the gate.

   ＜解答＞ enter

1199. I wouldn't have paid the money unless I (would have/had) owed it.

   ＜解答＞ had

1200. You might have enjoyed yourself if you (had/would have) gone with us.
＜解答＞ had

1201. The woman could explain these sentences if she (was/were) a teacher.
＜解答＞ were

1202. He (can/could) use the machine unless it is broken.
＜解答＞ can

1203. He (didn't understand/wouldn't have understood) you unless you had spoken slowly.
＜解答＞ wouldn't have understood

1204. Plants (wouldn't/don't) grow if the sun didn't shine.
＜解答＞ wouldn't

1205. If dinner (were/was) ready, I'd eat now.
＜解答＞ were

1206. He (wouldn't/doesn't) change his mind unless he were wrong.
＜解答＞ wouldn't

1207. Dicovered many years ago, (we find uranium/uranium is) a useful metal.
＜解答＞ uranium is

1208. Watching the slides carefully, (many familiar scenes appeared/we saw many familiar scenes).
＜解答＞ we saw many familiar scenes

1209. Having traveled at a high speed, (the motorist was issued a ticket/a ticket was issued to the motorist).
＜解答＞ the motorist was issued a ticket

1210. With a great deal of effort, (his course were passed/he passed his courses).
＜解答＞ he passed his courses

1211. While cooking dinner, (her finger was burned badly/she burned her finger badly).
＜解答＞ she burned her finger badly

1212. By looking in the telephone book, (his number can be found/you can find his number).

<解答>　you can find his number

1213. To dance well, (one needs practice/practice is needed).

<解答>　one needs practice

1214. Hurrying to class, (an accident happened/I had an accident) in my car.

<解答>　I had an accident

1215. After considering the plan for several days, (it was adopted/we adopted it).

<解答>　we adopted it

1216. When sick, (see/you should see) a doctor at once.

<解答>　you should see

1217. If not eaten, (you should throw away the dessert/the dessert should be thrown away).

<解答>　the dessert should be thrown away

1218. Shopping in the department store, (I noticed a pretty blouse/a pretty blouse came to my attention).

<解答>　I noticed a pretty blouse

1219. A busy person can't stand (to wait/waiting) in line.

<解答>　waiting

1220. Students must practice (using/to use) different words.

<解答>　using

1221. Would you please stop (to talk/talking) so loudly ?

<解答>　talking

1222. Do you hope (getting/to get) your degree by next year ?

<解答>　to get

1223. I hesitate (to say/saying) what I mean.

<解答>　to say

1224. Birds have to learn (to use/using) their wings.

<解答>　to use

1225. Can that student demand (to see/seeing) his grades ?

<解答>　to see

1226. My father is planning (to change/changing) jobs shortly.

   <解答> to change

1227. Did the cook remember (to add/adding) salt ?

   <解答> to add

1228. Almost everyone loves (have / having) free time.

   <解答> having

1229. The homesick child started (thinking/think) about his family.

   <解答> thinking

1230. I'm afraid (drive/to drive) alone at night.

   <解答> to drive

1231. Citizens ought to feel lucky (being/to be) able to vote.

   <解答> to be

1232. I'm looking for someone qualified (to type/typing) a thesis.

   <解答> to type

1233. Would you let me (use/to use) your pencil.

   <解答> use

1234. The company made the customer (pay/to pay) his bill.

   <解答> pay

1235. I had an electrician (repair/to repair) the wiring.

   <解答> repair

1236. I heard John (knocking/knock) at the door.

   <解答> knock

1237. Have you ever seen (a tiger's/a tiger) attaching a human being ?

   <解答> a tiger's

1238. Have you ever seen a tiger (to attack/attack) a human being ?

   <解答> attack

1239. Did you notice the car (to move/move) ?

   <解答> move

1240. Parents enjoy watching their (children/children's) playing.

   <解答> children

1241. Why do you dislike (me/my) cooking ?

<解答>　my

1242. I can't remember the (teacher/teacher's) announcing a test.

<解答>　teacher's

1243. Will you forgive (us/our) leaving early ?

<解答>　our

1244. (Paul's/Paul) winning the race surprised everyone.

<解答>　Paul's

1245. The movie is not worth (you/your) paying four dollars to see.

<解答>　your

1246. I won't insist on (his/him) wearing formal clothes.

<解答>　his

1247. The doctor has recommended (my father/my facther's) having an operation.

<解答>　my father's

1248. Every (citizen's/citizen) casting a vote is important.

<解答>　citizen's

1249. The boss excused (his secretary/his secretary's) failing to come to work.

<解答>　his secretary's

1250. Does the bed needed (to make/to be made) ?

<解答>　to be made

1251. My pencil needed (to sharpen/sharpening).

<解答>　sharpening

1252. He had knocked at the door and (rang/rung) the doorbell for ten minutes before someone answered.

<解答>　rung

1253. Had I (drove/driven) eight miles an hour, I would have been arrested.

<解答>　driven

1254. He has made and (broken/broke) promises to his friends all of his life.

<解答>　broken

1255. Having (spoken/spoke) to the audience for an hour, the speaker left the auditorium.

　　<解答> spoken

1256. It (only took/took only) two days to get there by train.

　　<解答> took only

1257. He was hoping to (by the end of the year find a job/a job by the end of the year).

　　<解答> a job by the end of the year

1258. I (nearly saw/saw nearly) 100 bears at the zoo.

　　<解答> saw nearly

1259. (To logically think/To think logically) in English is my goal.

　　<解答> To think logically

1260. The tiger (A. which came from Africa escaped from the cage/B. escaped from the cage which came from Africa).

　　<解答> A

1261. He was asked (to later sharpen/to sharpen) his pencil later.

　　<解答> to sharpen

1262. The carpenter makes furniture (of any size for people/for people of any size).

　　<解答> of any size for people

1263. The school children learned (A. In 1492 that columbus had discovered America/B. the Columbus had discovered America in 1492).

　　<解答> B

1264. A. Hiding in the bushes the policeman found the robber.

　　B. The policeman found the robber hiding in the bushes.

　　<解答> B

1265. The mansion (A. which the governor lives in was constructed by a new company/B. was constructed by a new company which the governor lives in).

　　<解答> A

1266. A. The vicuna has beautiful, silky hair which lives high in the mountains of Peru./B. The vicuna, which lives high in the mountains of Peru, has beautiful, silky hair.

＜解答＞ B

1267. A. Jumping from branch to branch, I was fascinated by a squirrel.

 B. I was fascinated by a squirrel jumping from branch to branch.

 ＜解答＞ B

1268. Lying on the beach were a towel, a red ball, and (broken/a broken) tennis racket.

 ＜解答＞ a broken

1269. He is both interested in and (dedicated to/dedicated) cancer research.

 ＜解答＞ dedicated to

1270. Laziness in people always (has/has been) and always will be one of my pet peeves.

 ＜解答＞ has been

1271. The traffic in New Orleans is heavier (than/than that of) Baton Rouge.

 ＜解答＞ than that of

1272. Teaching young children is not so different from (teaching teenagers / teenagers).

 ＜解答＞ teaching teenagers

1273. The day is dark, (with cloudy skies and a high humidity/cloudy, and humid).

 ＜解答＞ cloudy, and humid

1274. I read Hegel for the profound ideas in his philosophy (but not/but not for) his style of writing.

 ＜解答＞ but not for

1275. He was not only sympathetic (but also considerate/but also knew when to be considerate).

 ＜解答＞ but also considerate

1276. He was successful both as a church architect and (a poet/writing poetry).

 ＜解答＞ a poet

1277. I was concered about the price (of the car and if it was comfortable/and the comfort of the car).

<解答> and the comfort of the car

1278. A. Neither does he speak Spanish nor Helen.

B. Neither he nor Helen speaks Spanish.

<解答> B

1279. John decided to go to the university rather than (a job/to get a job).

<解答> to get a job

1280. He is a poor teacher, (but who/but he) treats his students fairly.

<解答> but he

1281. A . The vicuna is a timid animal and which lives in Peru.

B. The vicuna is an animal which is timid and which lives in Peru.

<解答> B

1282. I am studying the sources (of educational theory and how educational theory has evolved/and the evolution of educational theory).

<解答> and the evolution of educational theory

1283. In his hands he was holding a book and (interesting magazine/an interesting magazine).

<解答> an interesting magazine

1284. A. Not only did he enjoy the movie but also the play.

B. He enjoyed not only the movie but also the play.

<解答> B

1285. Playing tennis is more strenuous than (to ride a bicycle/riding a bicycle).

<解答> riding a bicycle

1286. Their homeland was cold and (mountainous/with many mountains).

<解答> mountainous

1287. She wanted the roof repaired and (to paint the fence/the fence painted).

<解答> the fence painted

1288. John Higgenbothan is a man (A. who has many ideas and who knows how to express them/B. of many ideas and who knows how to express them).

<解答> A

1289. For my birthday he gave me a watch (and which/which) I really like.

＜解答＞ which

1290. I learned that he was young, (but/but that) he was, nevertheless, ambitious.

＜解答＞ but that

1291. They said that they (didn't meet/hadn't met) him before.

＜解答＞ hadn't met

1292. I was surprised to learn that she (was/had been) injured in an accident.

＜解答＞ had been

1293. The robber wouldn't say where he (had spent/spent) all the money.

＜解答＞ had spent

1294. The librarian wanted to know where I (lost/had lost) the book.

＜解答＞ had lost

1295. Mr. Smith (just left/had just left) when his wife called.

＜解答＞ had just left

1296. He asked me what countries I (visited/had visited).

＜解答＞ had visited

1297. The clerk assured me that she (had told/told) the manager about my complaint.

＜解答＞ had told

1298. The little girl asked what (had happened/happened) to her dog.

＜解答＞ had happened

1299. We found out that our friend (went/had gone) to California.

＜解答＞ had gone

1300. When I saw him later, he (gained/had gained) over fifty pounds.

＜解答＞ had gained

1301. She was hurt to learn that her boyfriend (forgot/had forgotten) her birthday.

＜解答＞ had forgotten

1302. I discovered that someone (had drunk/drank) all the milk.

＜解答＞ had drunk

1303. It (already began/had already begun) to rain when we started for the beach.

＜解答＞ had already begun

1304. The senator declared that he (voted/had voted) for the new amendment.

　　＜解答＞ had voted

1305. (Eating/Having eaten) lunch, he took a nap.

　　＜解答＞ Having eaten

1306. (Driving/Having driven) for ten hours, we stopped to rest.

　　＜解答＞ Having driven

1307. My mother (would have liked/would like) to have been in Florida last week.

　　＜解答＞ would like

1308. She is happy (to meet/to have met) John when he was here.

　　＜解答＞ to have met

1309. I would have been afraid (to have touched/to touch) the lion at the zoo yesterday.

　　＜解答＞ to touch

1310. Where (is he/has he been) all day ?

　　＜解答＞ has he been

1311. I (bought/have bought) a new hat last weekend.

　　＜解答＞ bought

1312. They (are waiting/have been waiting) in the hall for half an hour.

　　＜解答＞ have been waiting

1313. I (haven't seen/don't see) John since last Monday.

　　＜解答＞ haven't seen

1314. The foreign student (hasn't met/doesn't meet) many Americans so far.

　　＜解答＞ hasn't met

1315. What (are you/have you been) doing since yesterday ?

　　＜解答＞ have you been

1316. He (has liked/likes) me ever since we met.

　　＜解答＞ has liked

1317. The girl (has been practicing/is practicing) the piano since early this morning.

　　＜解答＞ has been practicing

1318. Shakespeare (wrote/has written) many dramas.

　　＜解答＞　wrote

1319. (Have you written/Did you write) your composition last night ?

　　＜解答＞　Did you write

1320. He's looking for a wife, but he (doesn't find/hasn't found) one yet.

　　＜解答＞　hasn't found

1321. I (am already speaking/have already spoken) to her about that matter.

　　＜解答＞　have already spoken

1322. They (don't see/haven't seen) a movie in a year.

　　＜解答＞　haven't seen

1323. I still (don't learn/haven't learned) to speak English very well.

　　＜解答＞　haven't learned

1324. Oswald assassinated President John Kennedy. (This/This crime) shocked the world.

　　＜解答＞　This crime

1325. Mr. Young said that he would sell his farm at a very cheap price. (It/This statement) surprised all of the members of the Farm Bureau.

　　＜解答＞　This statement

1326. In college (you/one) has to study more than he does in high school.

　　＜解答＞　one

1327. When John was painting the garage, some of (it/the paint) spilled on his pants.

　　＜解答＞　the paint

1328. In Chicago (they/the people) have snow during the winter.

　　＜解答＞　the people

1329. (In the newspaper it said/The newspaper reported) that a new tax law had been passed.

　　＜解答＞　The newspaper reported

1330. Iowa, (that/which) lies in the north-central section of the United States, is between the Mississippi and Missouri river.

　　＜解答＞　which

1331. The Iowa country was first visited in 1673 by Joliet and Marquette, (that/who) were French explorers.

<解答> who

1332. The impala, (which/that) is one of the fastest and most graceful of antelopes, is found wild only in Africa.

<解答> which

1333. Kentucky was the home of Abraham Lincoln, (who/that) was president during the Civil War.

<解答> who

1334. The chief city of Hungary is Budapest, to (which/that) great damage was done during World War II.

<解答> which

1335. Some important discoveries about gravitation were made by Sir Issac Newton, (who/that) was a seventeenth-century scientist.

<解答> who

1336. Most of the world's supply of dates comes from Iraq, (that/which) is rapidly becoming an important modern country.

<解答> which

1337. After the bell rings, it (is/was) time to close the door.

<解答> is

1338. When I spoke to him, he (was/is) just getting ready to leave.

<解答> was

1339. He had serious operation while he (was/is) in the hospital.

<解答> was

1340. Like almost all teachers, she was well prepared and never (comes/came) to class late.

<解答> came

1341. When you got home, (do/did) you notice what time it was ?

<解答> did

1342. If you had told her that she was wrong, she (would be/would have been) angry.

<解答>　would have been

1343. Everyone in class know that the examination (was/is) going to include six chapters.

<解答>　was

1344. As soon as I finish biology, I (take/will take) chemistry.

<解答>　will take

1345. I will answer the phone if it (rings/rang).

<解答>　rings

1346. When we reached the station, it (is/was) well after midnight.

<解答>　was

1347. That essay is very timely even though it (was/is) written two hundred years ago.

<解答>　was

1348. When Napoleon (lost/loses) the Battle of Waterloo, he was exiled to the island of St. Helena.

<解答>　lost

1349. I see that you (wear/are wearing) your new coat today.

<解答>　are wearing

1350. When I go to work, I generally (am meeting/meet) many school children.

<解答>　meet

1351. He needs to wear clothes today because it (freezes/is freezing).

<解答>　is freezing

1352. Policemen (issue/are issuing) tickets to speeders.

<解答>　issue

1353. They (are sitting/sit) in class everyday for several hours.

<解答>　sit

1354. Why (do you wash/are you washing) your car this morning ?

<解答>　are you washing

1355. I almost always think in English, but today I (think/am thinking) in my native language.

<解答>　am thinking

1356. He (sleeps/is sleeping) because he worked very hard this morning.

<解答>　is sleeping

1357. I (listen/am listening), but I cannot hear a sound.

<解答>　am listening

1358. How often (are you studying/do you study) in the library ?

<解答>　do you study

1359. Look! That woman (is running/runs) to catch the bus.

<解答>　is running

1360. When the student wants to ask a question, he (is raising/raises) his hand.

<解答>　raises

1361. Bad students usually (do not work/are not working) hard.

<解答>　do not work

1362. The man, as well as his wife and children, (were/was) injured in the accident.

<解答>　was

1363. A crate of apples and oranges (has/have) been delivered to our doorstep.

<解答>　has

1364. The man and his assistant (are/is) pleased with the new office.

<解答>　are

1365. Either the students or the teacher (has/have) made a mistake.

<解答>　has

1366. Buried under the floorboards (is/are) the murdered man.

<解答>　is

1367. The best time to take a nap (is/are) the two hours after lunch.

<解答>　is

1368. The jury (disagrees/disagree) on the verdict.

<解答>　disagrees

1369. Thirty dollars (are/is) too much to pay for that purse.

<解答>　is

1370. The number of students who pass (is/are) increasing.

　　　＜解答＞　is

1371. The acoustice of the building (is/are) good.

　　　＜解答＞　are

1372. One of the men who (are/is) being considered for the job is from this university.

　　　＜解答＞　are

1373. Economics, my major, (is/are) difficult.

　　　＜解答＞　is

1374. A number of students (fails/fail) every test.

　　　＜解答＞　fail

1375. Ten miles (is/are) not far to go for a delicious meal.

　　　＜解答＞　is

1376. There (is/are) at least fifteen angry demonstrators outside.

　　　＜解答＞　are

1377. The parent or the children (inherit/inherits) the estate.

　　　＜解答＞　inherit

1378. My friend and teacher (is/are) my mother.

　　　＜解答＞　is

1379. Every one of the employees (is/are) angry about the new contract.

　　　＜解答＞　is

1380. One of the students in the class (is/are) absent today.

　　　＜解答＞　is

1381. The conselor has insisted that Tommy (take/takes) time to relax.

　　　＜解答＞　take

1382. Did the general urge that his troops (fight/fought) ?

　　　＜解答＞　fight

1383. My father suggested that ((didn't buy/not buy) a used car.

　　　＜解答＞　not buy

1384. It is essential that each camper (bring/brings) his own equipment.

　　＜解答＞　bring

1385. Was It recommended that the young woman (not drive/didn't drive) after dark ?

　　＜解答＞　not drive

1386. It seemed urgent that the meeting (began/begin) immediately.

　　＜解答＞　begin

1387. Your request that the test (is delayed/be delayed) has been denied.

　　＜解答＞　be delayed

1388. I wish you (had called/would have called) me yesterday.

　　＜解答＞　had called

1389. I wish it (rained/rains) more in this area during the spring.

　　＜解答＞　rained

1390. I wish I (knew/had known) you ten years ago.

　　＜解答＞　had known

1391. I wish you (won't interrupt/wouldn't interrupt) me while I'm talking.

　　＜解答＞　wouldn't interrupt

1392. The student wishes that he (took/had taken) English in high school.

　　＜解答＞　had taken

1393. Don't you wish you (can dance/could dance) better ?

　　＜解答＞　could dance

1394. The secretary wishes that she (has/had) time to type the letter now.

　　＜解答＞　had

1395. She wishes that she (was/were) a good actress.

　　＜解答＞　were

1396. A. I think that Being There is Peter Sellers' best movie, superior to all others.

　　B. I think that Being There is Peter Sellers' best movie.

　　＜解答＞　B

1397. The novel was neither interesting nor (was it well written/well written).

　　＜解答＞　well written

1398. There are (various and sundry/various) reasons why one should avoid discussing religion.

＜解答＞ various

1399. It was (clearly evident/evident) that the grass had been cut.

＜解答＞ evident

1400. I picked up the heavy tools with my (two hands/hands).

＜解答＞ hands

1401. A. There is a society called the Audubon Society, which was named in honor of John Audubon, the great artist./B. The Audubon Society was named in honor of John Audubon, the great artist.

＜解答＞ B

1402. A. Regarding the subject of laws governing motorists, many people feel that the speed limit should be increased to sixty-five miles per hour./B. Many people feel that the speed limit should be increased to sixty-five miles per hour.

＜解答＞ B

1403. A. The famous singing group, " The Rolling Stones, " is known internationally throughout the world./B. " The Rolling Stones " is an internationally known singing group.

＜解答＞ B

1404. A. The bridge stretched across the vast swampland, and the bridge was twenty-five miles long./B. The twenty-five-mile-long bridge stretched across the vast swampland.

＜解答＞ B

1405. A. She is a tennis player who plays tennis regularly.

B. She plays tennis regularly.

＜解答＞ B

1406. A. Sir Thomas More wrote Utopia.

B. Sir Thomas More was a writer who wrote Utopia.

＜解答＞ A

1407. He spoke (A. at the meeting knowledgeably/B. knowledgeably at the meeting) this morning.

<解答> B

1408. A. I read quickly the letter from my parents.

B. I read the letter from my parents quickly.

<解答> B

1409. A. The Arab speaks very well English./B. The Arab speaks English very well.

<解答> B

1410. My husband prefers to eat (his lunch at home/at home his lunch) at noon.

<解答> his lunch at home

1411. A. the family came to the United States by boat in 1975.

B. The family came in 1975 to the United States by boat.

<解答> A

1412. Do you want to go (to the movies tonight/tonight to the movies) ?

<解答> to the movies tonight

1413. A. She does completely her assignments every night.

B. She does her assignments completely every hight.

<解答> B

1414. I (forget sometimes/sometimes forget) my phone number.

<解答> sometimes forget

1415. The highways (are usually crowded/usually are crowded) on the weekend.

<解答> are usually crowded

1416. Almost (never/never does) he iron his own clothes.

<解答> never does

1417. Not only (he broke/did he break) two glasses, but also he left the table dirty.

<解答> did he break

1418. Do you know why (is he/he is) so angry ?

<解答> he is

1419. He doesn't know when (will he be/he will be) here again.

<解答> he will be

1420. I'm never quite sure whom (can I trust/I can trust).

<解答> I can trust

1421. Can you tell me where (is his house/his house is) ?

<解答> his house is

1422. We (have just finished/just have finished) eating.

<解答> have just finished

1423. Rarelly (have I been/I have been) to court.

<解答> have I been

1424. Hardly ever (they attend/do they attend) church.

<解答> do they attend

1425. Nowhere in this city (you will find/will you find) high fashion.

<解答> will you find

1426. It is unclear how (did he escape/he escaped).

<解答> he escaped

1427. Please show me how (this machine works/does this machine work).

<解答> this machine works

1428. I need to know what time (is it/it is).

<解答> it is

1429. I wonder why (did he tell/he told) a lie.

<解答> he told

1430. You and I (are/am) happy.

<解答> are

1431. You and John (is/are) teachers.

<解答> are

1432. John and Mary (is/are) from San Francisco.

<解答> are

1433. Are the students busy ? Yes, (they are/they're not).

<解答> they are

1434. Are the books in Mexico ? No, they (aren't/are).

<解答> aren't

1435. John (practice/practices) in the morning, and we practice in the afternoon.

<解答> practices

1436. Do Mr. and Mrs. Lee like tea ? Yes, they (are/do).

    ＜解答＞ do

1437. Alice (seldom studies/studies seldom) at night.

    ＜解答＞ seldom studies

1438. Does John always (work/works) in the morning ?

    ＜解答＞ work

1439. Do you ever have cornflakes for breakfast ? Yes, (often/ever).

    ＜解答＞ often

1440. The teacher has coffee (in the afternoon in that building/in that building in the afternoon).

    ＜解答＞ in that building in the afternoon

1441. Does John study (at the library every day/every day at the library) ?

    ＜解答＞ at the library every day

1442. Did Mary read the book ? No, She's going to (read/reading) the book tomorrow.

    ＜解答＞ read

1443. No, None of the students (is/are) sick.

    ＜解答＞ are

1444. Not much of the bread (is/are) good. Only a little of it is good.

    ＜解答＞ is

1445. Not all of the books are here. Only some of them (are/is) here.

    ＜解答＞ are

1446. Would you please close the window. Yes, (I'm/I'd be) glad to.

    ＜解答＞ I'd be

1447. No, let's (not/don't) go to the movies. Let's watch television.

    ＜解答＞ not

1448. No, he's going to eat dinner at a restaurant (tomorrow/yesterday).

    ＜解答＞ tomorrow

1449. Yes, he taught her some, but he didn't teach me (any/some).

    ＜解答＞ any

1450. When we were in London we (could/were able to) visit the British Museum.
＜解答＞ were able to

1451. You must (can/be able to) run fast.
＜解答＞ be able to

1452. What did John go to (the store for/the store) ?
＜解答＞ the store for

1453. The quality of this shirt is (the same as/as same as) the quality of that one.
＜解答＞ the same as

1454. The man (whose/that) car John bought came yesterday.
＜解答＞ whose

1455. It began to rain while I (was watching/watched) the baseball game.
＜解答＞ was watching

1456. I (drank/was drinking) some tomato juice when I dropped the book.
＜解答＞ was drinking

1457. When visiting a foreing country, you must (adapt/adopt) yourself to the customs practiced there.
＜解答＞ adapt

1458. The Grays plan to (adopt/adapt) several hard-to-place children.
＜解答＞ adopt

1459. I resent your (allusion/illusion) to my cooking as comparable with MacDonalad's.
＜解答＞ allusion

1460. You have the (allusion/illusion) that I enjoy classical music; I don't.
＜解答＞ illusion

1461. Many a would-be-bride has been left at the (alter/altar).
＜解答＞ altar

1462. Would it be inconvenient for you to (alter/altar) your plans for this weekend ?
＜解答＞ alter

1463. Ira was (angry at/angry with) the thought of working overtime.
＜解答＞ angry at

1464. Ira was (angry with/angry at) his boss for insistening that Ira work overtime.
　　＜解答＞　angry with

1465. I am (anxious/eager) about the diagnosis.
　　＜解答＞　anxious

1466. I am (eager/anxious) to see your new car.
　　＜解答＞　eager

1467. The (ascent/assent) to the tower was frighteningly steep.
　　＜解答＞　ascent

1468. Because I value his opinion, I will not go ahead with the project without his (assent/ascent).
　　＜解答＞　assent

1469. Our youngest child was (borne/born) last month.
　　＜解答＞　born

1470. John has (born/borne) the burden by himself for long enough.
　　＜解答＞　borne

1471. Because he did not (brake/break) in time, Herman crashed into the tree.
　　＜解答＞　brake

1472. If you are not careful, you will (break/brake) that dish.
　　＜解答＞　break

1473. Some fortunate people (can/may) arrange their time to include work and pleasure.
　　＜解答＞　can

1474. You (may/can) hunt deer only during certain seasons.
　　＜解答＞　may

1475. I find this (course/coarse) fabric to be abrasive.
　　＜解答＞　coarse

1476. That is an acceptable (course/coarse) of action.
　　＜解答＞　course

1477. I'd like to (compliment/complements) you for doing such a thorough job.
　　＜解答＞　compliment

1478. Rice nicely (complements/compliment) a chicken dinner.

　　＜解答＞　complements

1479. Tom is (continually/continuously) late.

　　＜解答＞　continually

1480. The river runs (continuously/continually) through several towns.

　　＜解答＞　continuously

1481. Our neighbor has just been elected to the town (council/counsel).

　　＜解答＞　council

1482. The troubled man sought his friend's (counsel/council).

　　＜解答＞　counsel

1483. Because the defendant had a good alibi, his story seemed (credible/creditable).

　　＜解答＞　credible

1484. As a result of many hours of hand work, Joe presented a (creditable/credible) report.

　　＜解答＞　creditable

1485. Suely is so (credulous/credible) that one could sell her the Brooklyn Bridge.

　　＜解答＞　credulous

1486. His unusal recipe called for (currant/current) jelly.

　　＜解答＞　currant

1487. Because the (currant/current) was swift, the canoe was difficult to maneuver.

　　＜解答＞　current

1488. Although he did not state it directly, the candidate (inferred/implied) that his opponent was dishonest.

　　＜解答＞　implied

1489. From the mayor's constructive suggestions, the townsfolk (implied/inferred) that he was trying his best to do a good job.

　　＜解答＞　inferred

1490. I'll need one more (lead/led) pipe to complete this plumbing job.

　　＜解答＞　lead

1491. John was unfamiliar with that route, so John (lead/led) the way.

<解答> led

1492. The (manor/manner), or landed estate, dastes back to feudal times in England.

<解答> manor

1493. They don't like the (manner/manor) in which you responded to my sincere question.

<解答> manner

1494. The young man was not allowed to enter the bar because he was a (minor/miner).

<解答> minor

1495. The coal (minors/miners) were trapped during the vave-in.

<解答> miners

1496. Because of Ed's high (moral/morale) standards, he returned the wallet to its owner.

<解答> moral

1497. Because the war was immoral, the (morale/moral) of the troops was low.

<解答> morale

1498. When we drove past the skunk, the car was filled with a (nauseous/nauseated) odor.

<解答> nauseous

1499. The odor of the skunk (nauseated/nauseous) Sara.

<解答> nauseated

1500. The amount of paint needed to finish the job would fill a one gallon (pail/pale).

<解答> pail

1501. Because of her long illness, Maria's complexion was very (pail/pale).

<解答> pale

1502. Older children frequently (persecute/prosecute) their younger siblings.

<解答> persecute

1503. If you do not return the stolen money, you will be (prosecuted/persecuted).

<解答> prosecuted

1504. The items written in a young girl's diary are very (personal/personnel).

<解答> personal

1505. When applying for a job at a large company, you must go to the (personnel/personal) office.

<解答> personnel

1506. Theater seats are most often (stationery/stationary).

<解答> stationary

1507. When I write letters, I always use my engraved (stationery/stationary).

<解答> stationery

1508. The (vain/vane) man peered at his reflection in every window as he strolled down the street.

<解答> vain

1509. A rooster is the traditional weather (vain/vane) symbol.

<解答> vane

1510. (Veins/Vanes) are passageways which carry deoxygenated blood to the heart.

<解答> Veins

1511. (Veil/Vale) is an uncommonly used synonym for valley.

<解答> Vale

1512. The mourning woman hid her grief behind her (veil/vale).

<解答> veil

1513. If you measure your (waist/waste) before you go to buy a pattern, you will avoid much confusion.

<解答> waist

1514. Don't (waste/waist) precious time gossiping on the phone.

<解答> waste

1515. A group of puzzled citizens (stand/stands) before the monument each day and reads the strange inscription written upon it.

<解答> stands

1516. Although measles (is/are) considered a childhood disease, often the disease itself, as well as the accompanying complications, proves serious to adults.

<解答> is

1517. The Communist party, as well as other political groups that despise capitalism, (is/are) controlled by those who live in wealth and comfort.
<解答> is

1518. There, but for the intervention of our parents, (goes/go) my friends and I.
<解答> goes

1519. The person in the city, as well as people in suburbs, often I (lives/live) in a complicated world, with many hours spent each day getting to and from work.
<解答> lives

1520. Who (are/is) the leaders or the captains of this unruly mob of protesters who are parading on the courthouse square ?
<解答> are

1521. Black-eyed peas and hog jowl, known as " hopping John " in the South, (have/has) become a New Year's Day tradition.
<解答> has

1522. There (exist/exists) unexlored regions and undeveloped tribes in South America.
<解答> exist

1523. Inside the fence (stand/stands) three markers which honor the three Indian chiefs who, each in his own way, were helpful to the settlers.
<解答> stand

1524. A multitude of eager listeners (were/was) standing within range of the speaker's voice, although neither she nor her followers was members of these peoples organization.
<解答> was

1525. Even though our team has different ideas concerning the championship, the members are united on one idea; that is, our team (is/are) to win.
<解答> is

1526. It is I, not they, who (demands/demand) an explanation.
<解答> demand

1527. Because it doesn't seem possible for our nation to perish, we sometimes forget that each of us (have/has) a distinctive role in its preservation.
　＜解答＞　has

1528. The writer, not the readers, (was/were) responsible for the impression that was conveyed.
　＜解答＞　was

1529. All members of the Board of Commissioners, as well as Mayor Hill, (deserve/deserves) credit for the successful pageant.
　＜解答＞　deserve

1530. The results of my continuous effort seem negligible, but you, having a very able assistant, (has/have) been more successful.
　＜解答＞　have

1531. Let's you and (I/me) volunteer for the job, as it's an interesting project.
　＜解答＞　I

1532. Roberta disapproved of (us/our) going, but we felt we understood the hazards better than her.
　＜解答＞　our

1533. I wanted you and (him/he) to find her.
　＜解答＞　him

1534. Martin and I will be going, and (he and she/him and her) are to join us.
　＜解答＞　he and she

1535. The teacher must decide for whether to give the work to John or (I/me).
　＜解答＞　me

1536. Every boy needs to take his swimming suit to the Tylers, as we may swim in (they're/their) pool.
　＜解答＞　their

1537. I don't know Michael as well as her, but I remember (his/him) coming to the club dance.
　＜解答＞　his

1538. Were they later than we, or were (us/we) girls on time ?
　　　<解答> we

1539. I should like to be her for many reasons, but I feel I am happier than (she/her).
　　　<解答> she

1540. They took us, Jean and me, to town; but it was Mrs. Smith (who/whom) brought us home.
　　　<解答> who

1541. If I (knew/had known) your parents, I would have visited them.
　　　<解答> had known

1542. The accountant who made the mistake looked as though she (was/were) very contrite.
　　　<解答> were

1543. When I reached the city, I found that I (lost/had lost) my purse.
　　　<解答> had lost

1544. I shall refuse every offer; you (shall/will) not change my mind by arguing.
　　　<解答> will

1545. Sometimes James acts as if I (was/were) responsible for his failure, although neither his frients nor I advise him in any undertaking.
　　　<解答> were

1546. He had studied French and Spanish and (completed/had completed) his English courses before he came to our school.
　　　<解答> had completed

1547. In the last chapter Tommy sets the prisoners free; but they, angry at their treatment, (shouted/shout) at their captors.
　　　<解答> shout

1548. Last year I (took/have taken) all my entrance examination.
　　　<解答> took

1549. Antonio demanded that his brother called home and (asks/asked) permission to make the purchase.
　　　<解答> asked

1550. The traveller stopped at the well and asked for a drink; but the farmer, with his two sons at his side, (order/ordered) him off the land.
　　＜解答＞　ordered

1551. Vilma told us that the people locked the dog in the car and (went/had gone) to the fair.
　　＜解答＞　went

1552. If I were that person, I would be sure I (looked/had looked) for the book before I bought a new one.
　　＜解答＞　had looked

1553. Everyone should be careful of her or his appearance, for one is often judged by the first impression that (she or he makes/they make).
　　＜解答＞　she or he makes

1554. The boy must understand what he reads if (he is/they are) to acquire knowledge.
　　＜解答＞　he is

1555. Although none of (us/we) dancers will make dancing a career, we especially Jame and I, are interested in the stage.
　　＜解答＞　us

1556. Having assured ourselves that the speaker was (she/her), we sent the members to judge her speech for themselves.
　　＜解答＞　she

1557. For (he/him) and us they have done much; now we must do for ourselves.
　　＜解答＞　him

1558. The person who can laugh at himself is one (who/whom) I think will overcome many obstacles.
　　＜解答＞　who

1559. Jack did the work himself, as no one else was as competent as (him/he).
　　＜解答＞　he

1560. We were excited over his winning, but we regretted (us/our) having lost.
　　＜解答＞　our

1561. The party planned for Stella and them was postponed when several (who/whom) they had invited became ill.

　＜解答＞ whom

1562. All of (those/them) who came were interested in us boys and wanted to do all that they could for us.

　＜解答＞ those

1563. Even though they are larger than I, I will work hard to show that I am as efficient as (they/them).

　＜解答＞ they

1564. If he and I can go, we will send our reservations to (those/them) who are in change.

　＜解答＞ those

1565. Athletics (was/were) given little stress as a part of the curriculum, and to no player was given honor and recognition.

　＜解答＞ werre

1566. There (stand/stands) the two statues; and each child, as well as adults, is reminded of the national heroes.

　＜解答＞ stand

1567. Although there are several recognizable dialects used in our country, no one of them (show/shows) a great difference in speech.

　＜解答＞ shows

1568. Her one aim and ambition is to rise higher than her uncle, who, with his three children, (has/have) amassed a fortune.

　＜解答＞ has

1569. When italics (is/are) used to emphasize a word, special efforts to understand the word is necessary.

　＜解答＞ are

1570. All must do the work for themselves, for each will differ in (her or his/their) choice of a subject and a method of presentation.

　＜解答＞ her or his

1571. After hours of deliberation, the jury gave its verdict; the man (who/whom) I think was guilty was acquitted.

＜解答＞ who

1572. Did you know that the chairperson was (she/her) when you asked Jack, Susan, and me to outline a course of study for you ?

＜解答＞ she

1573. Although we had waited six months (on/for) his decision, the final report did not please us.

＜解答＞ for

1574. He spoke (as/like) a true humantitarion speaks, but his words carried no conviction.

＜解答＞ like

1575. The play may have been interesting to you (and/but) I did not enjoy it.

＜解答＞ but

1576. (Besides/Beside) Ann and Fran, we will need three other leaders.

＜解答＞ Besides

1577. Everything that she stated was different (from/than) the ideas that we had thought important.

＜解答＞ from

1578. He has (either won/won either) the first or the second prize.

＜解答＞ won either

1579. Have you read (where/that) our commissioners are visiting the school again as they did last year ?

＜解答＞ that

1580. Many companies allow a discount, (providing/provided) the bill is paid in ten days.

＜解答＞ providing

1581. The work on the new courthouse cannot be completed (except/unless) more workers are hired.

＜解答＞ unless

1582. (Since/Being that) you do not need the book, may I use it ?

　　＜解答＞　Since

1583. I can play the piano well, (while/but) Helen sings better than I.

　　＜解答＞　but

1584. My parents, as well as my grandparents, (attend/attends) the small church which lies hidden in the thick grove beside the river.

　　＜解答＞　attend

1585. That kind of remark can produce hysteria; I, in addition to the other officers, (was/were) aware of this fact.

　　＜解答＞　was

1586. Her father, but not her mother, (know/knows) that she can work as well as either James or her cousin.

　　＜解答＞　knows

1587. We expected (to arrive/to have arrived) at noon, but all except Brenda and I were late.

　　＜解答＞　to have arrived

1588. I wonder if Lupe expects to have a (real/really) successful trip, as she must divide her time among several towns.

　　＜解答＞　really

1589. The boy looks like his father, and he works (as if/like) he were grown.

　　＜解答＞　as if

1590. (Most/Almost) all of us feel bad about his leaving.

　　＜解答＞　Almost

1591. She stood between Mother and me as we waited (in back of/behind) the curtain.

　　＜解答＞　behind

1592. The snow (lay/laid) deep in the fields, the silence grew deeper, and Pope, together with his cousins was finding the hours in the country very lonesome.

　　＜解答＞　laid

1593. Either the stage manager or one of her assistants (prepare/prepares) our script and has it ready when each of us arrives.

<解答> prepares

1594. What she doesn't know, in this case, may cause her much trouble, for none of her workers (have/has) told her about the strike.

<解答> has

1595. Membership in these clubs and social groups (seem/seems) important to many people in our city.

<解答> seems

1596. Not one of the girls (intend/intends) to enter college near her home.

<解答> intends

1597. " It was either (him/he) or I, " the thug answered with bravado.

<解答> he

1598. The number of hits (decline/declines) when the target is moved back.

<解答> declines

1599. Jorge (swang/swung) at the pinata as hard as he could.

<解答> swung

1600. You can't imagine how (bad/badly) I felt when I heard the report.

<解答> bad

1601. Placing all of her carefully prepared notes on the table, Yolanda spoke (with/to) the committee, allowing no one to interrupt her statements.

<解答> to

1602. The man whom I believe is the most capable has decided not to serve, and his refusing to take part has given the opposition the right to insist upon (its/their) candidate.

<解答> its

1603. Each boy thought of his own safety; all forgot (their/there) neighbors.

<解答> their

1604. He will never win the contest, although he has (most/almost) won it several times.

<解答> almost

1605. The couple (has only/only has) one child, and they are surely proud of her accomplishments.

＜解答＞ only has

1606. If I were sure of the date, I could secure tickets for (us/we) boys and for Ann and her.

＜解答＞ us

1607. You do not speak as (good/well) as he, but your singing is better.

＜解答＞ well

1608. If any boy calls, please tell him to sit in the lounge; (he/they) may entertain himself there.

＜解答＞ he

1609. A long line of cars, each of which was driven by a uniformed driver, blocked the street so that pedestrians, some of whom (were/was) already late for work, could not pass.

＜解答＞ were

1610. The coat were of a dark material which picks up lint and threads and (grow/grows) shiny with constant wear.

＜解答＞ grows

1611. As usall, you were right, but I, in addition to Jane and Gay, (believe/believes) that some changes should be made.

＜解答＞ believe

1612. Since I did not know (who/whom) Ella's substitute teacher was, I called the principal's office.

＜解答＞ whom

1613. Jack and Barbara were teamed up against Roberto and (I/me).

＜解答＞ me

1614. From the sound of the noise, the rear axle must be (broke/broken).

＜解答＞ broken

1615. Not every driver in these states (buy/buys) a license tag at the same time of year.

＜解答＞ buys

1616. It looks (like/as if) it will be a warm, sunny day.

　　＜解答＞　as if

1617. Although you are stronger than he, it was (he/him), not you, who offered to
carry the packages for Mother and me.

　　＜解答＞　he

1618. You don't know her as well as (me/I), but you are welcome to come with her
and me.

　　＜解答＞　me

1619. The author (who/whom) we like best is Poc, but we do not expect others to
select him as their favorite.

　　＜解答＞　whom

1620. You and I should purchase the land while (its/it's) still relatively cheap.

　　＜解答＞　it's

1621. Among the guests whom we expect is one woman whose life has been one of
service to others and of satisfaction to (her/herself).

　　＜解答＞　her

1622. The arrival of Manuel and Jack (doesn't/don't) necessarily mean that the basic
plan of our various compaigns is to be changed.

　　＜解答＞　doesn't

1623. When a number of citizens (express/expresses) the desire for a change, either
the mayor or the commissioners need to consider the matter.

　　＜解答＞　express

1624. One of her best traits is friendliness; but, as she is one of those who (is/are)
often in dreamland, everyone doesn't understand her.

　　＜解答＞　is

1625. People have found that (its/it's) harder to learn to live together than to learn to
fight each other.

　　＜解答＞　it's

1626. Many pioneers find life in South America a challenge as they, together with
other adventurers, (explore/explores) the dense jungles.

<解答>　explore

1627. I read in the paper (where/that) the money was to be divided among the three state colleges.

<解答>　that

1628. The reason for our tardiness was (because/that) the train was late; at eight it finally came into the station.

<解答>　that

1629. Although I cannot agree with you, I am willing to discuss the matter further and to (accept/except) expert opinion.

<解答>　accept

1630. Although we could (hardly/not hardly) understand his words, his gestures explained his meaning well.

<解答>　hardly

1631. This team will never win (unless/without) the players practice as they should.

<解答>　unless

1632. If you had spoken more softly, the bird would not have (flew/flown).

<解答>　flown

1633. Why he (ran/run) all the way home, we never knew.

<解答>　ran

1634. None of the robes had been (wore/worn) by the previous class.

<解答>　worn

1635. We could see the ruts where the heavy logs had been (drug/dragged).

<解答>　dragged

1636. Jim had shown his fear when he had (shrank/shrunk) back.

<解答>　shrunk

1637. Jan (dived/dove) from the highest tower and swam toward us.

<解答>　dived

1638. The big balloon (bursted/burst) just we came into the pavilion.

<解答>　burst

1639. There (is/are) apples, oranges, and plums in the basket.

<解答>　are

1640. Neither Tom nor Jerry (was/were) surprised at the victory.

<解答>　was

1641. Where (is/are) the new tools kept now ?

<解答>　are

1642. There (is/are) not many people ready to accept the responsibility for that job.

<解答>　are

1643. The number of cases of measles (has/have) decreased since last year.

<解答>　has

1644. (Is/Are) each of girls to wear a costume ?

<解答>　Is

1645. Both of the deer (is/are) in the pen.

<解答>　are

1646. Washington, with his contemporaries, (has/have) been greatly honored.

<解答>　has

1647. (Was/Were) you with the girls' basketball team ?

<解答>　Were

1648. New developments in science (interest/interests) all of us.

<解答>　interest

1649. Many people (has/have) found themselves in just such a predicament.

<解答>　have

1650. The Scouts (agree/agrees) on the next project.

<解答>　agree

1651. Everybody (was/were) delighted.

<解答>　was

1652. Either basketball or tennis (is/are) played each day.

<解答>　is

1653. The choir (is/are) to sing tonight in the annual program.

<解答>　is

1654. A herd of wild horses (race/races) across the plains each day.

<解答>　races

1655. Neither the boy nor the girl (cheers/cheer) the rival from Stanton High.

<解答>　cheers

1656. Every one of the children (behave/behaves) well at all times.

<解答>　behaves

1657. (Tom's and Bill's/Tom and Bill's) boats are at the pier.

<解答>　Tom's and Bill's

1658. At one of the (rallys/rallies), he spoke against the new law.

<解答>　rallies

1659. She wanted the two large (trout's/trouts') heads to be mounted.

<解答>　trout's

1660. (Ken Bass'/Ken Bass's) strange sense of humor did not please his family.

<解答>　Ken Bass'

1661. In the room, we saw three (shelfs/shelves) of old-fashioned shaving mugs.

<解答>　shelves

1662. The English (lord's/lords') seats in Parliament are inherited.

<解答>　lords'

1663. The (ships'/ship's) cargo was seized by the harbor officials.

<解答>　ship's

1664. We watched in amazement as the (salmon/salmons) fifted their bodies.

<解答>　salmons

1665. Every (schoolchild's/schoolchilds') fingerprints were taken.

<解答>　schoolchild's

1666. The (men's/mens') class will hold its banquet on Thursday night.

<解答>　men's

1667. A (weeks/week's) supply of food is kept in each locker.

<解答>　week's

1668. We laughed at the (monkies/monkeys) as they swung on the limb.

<解答>　monkeys

1669. The only coat that I could find was (Juanita's/Juanitas').

＜解答＞ Juanita's

1670. On the boat I met three Russians and four (Germen/Germans).

＜解答＞ Germans

1671. The (crowds'/crowd's) enthusiasm was evident in their rapt attention.

＜解答＞ crowd's

1672. The antlers both (deer/deers) were mounted and placed on exhibition.

＜解答＞ deer

1673. Several million (dollars'/dollar's) worth of surplus farm products were shipped to the East.

＜解答＞ dollars'

1674. This book is more interesting than (any/any other) that he has written.

＜解答＞ any other

1675. His parents are (wealthier/more wealthy) than mine.

＜解答＞ wealthier

1676. This is the (worse/worst) day that we have had this winter.

＜解答＞ worst

1677. Ned an I (sure/surely) had a wonderful summer.

＜解答＞ surely

1678. Anita's solution is (more correct/more nearly correct) than his.

＜解答＞ more correct

1679. Step more (closer/closely) to the fence, please.

＜解答＞ closely

1680. The big ball in the baby's playpen is (very round/round).

＜解答＞ round

1681. Her answer was (correct/most correct).

＜解答＞ correct

1682. The grass is (greener/greenest) in the other person's field.

＜解答＞ greener

1683. The lovely old vase was (unique/most unique).

<解答>　unique

1684. He spells (worse/worst) than any of his classmates.

<解答>　worse

1685. Buy a newspaper and bring (it/them) home.

<解答>　it

1686. Marlene went to the party but (she/her) didn't stay long.

<解答>　she

1687. Pedro wanted to see the polar bears, camels, and tropical birds, (which/they) were at the zoo.

<解答>　which

1688. When Mark, Steven, Teresa, and Barbara became eighteen, (they/them) registered to vote.

<解答>　they

1689. The plates broke when (it/they) fell.

<解答>　they

1690. The lamp hit the table when (the lamp/it) was knocked over.

<解答>　the lamp

1691. Everyone at the party looked (beautifully/beautiful).

<解答>　beautiful

1692. Those shoes are her (favorite/favoritely) ones.

<解答>　favorite

1693. The librarian spoke (softly/soft).

<解答>　softly

1694. Jackie Onassis is (extremely/extreme) rich.

<解答>　extremely

1695. The mayor campaigned (throughout/through) the city.

<解答>　throughout

1696. The strainer (for/to) the sink is broken.

<解答>　for

1697. The accident occurred (about/to) eight o'clock.

　　　＜解答＞　about

1698. Alan's father (and/or) mother are divorced.

　　　＜解答＞　and

1699. Is your favorite song at the end (and/or) in the middle of the record ?

　　　＜解答＞　or

1700. You may swim in the pool (but/and) don't stay long.

　　　＜解答＞　but

1701. Everyone (but/of) Sam was invited to the wedding.

　　　＜解答＞　but

1702. The Orioles won the pennant (also/but) the Angels came close to winning.

　　　＜解答＞　but

1703. Harry has (but/enough) ten dollars left in his bank account.

　　　＜解答＞　but

1704. Every life has its (ups/up) and downs.

　　　＜解答＞　ups

1705. Attempting to save Annie, the fireman ran for the door, dragging her (behind/out).

　　　＜解答＞　behind

1706. From his room, (he/they) could see the park.

　　　＜解答＞　he

1707. The children loved the man (who/whom) sold ice cream.

　　　＜解答＞　who

1708. Before the race, (the jockeys/they) inspected their horses.

　　　＜解答＞　the jockeys

1709. When the rain stopped, (it/the air) was cooler.

　　　＜解答＞　the air

1710. During the riot, (several/few) people got hurt.

　　　＜解答＞　several

1711. When she won the lottery, (Mrs. Lee/He) shouted with joy.

　　＜解答＞ Mrs. Lee

1712. We got the day (off/of).

　　＜解答＞ off

1713. (The fire/When the fire) was put out.

　　＜解答＞ The fire

1714. (It rained/Because it rained) this early morning.

　　＜解答＞ It rained

1715. While the washing machine was broken, (we/it) couldn't wash anything.

　　＜解答＞ we

1716. Jack abandoned the car (which/who) had two flat tires.

　　＜解答＞ which

1717. The job was offered to Ann (because/that) she was the best qualified.

　　＜解答＞ because

1718. My new neighbor is the one (who/whom) is waving.

　　＜解答＞ who

1719. Woody Allen's new film is the funniest movie that he has made (yet/already).

　　＜解答＞ already

1720. The child giggled (during/while) he was asleep.

　　＜解答＞ while

1721. Please tell me (that/what) this is all about.

　　＜解答＞ what

1722. Thurmon Munson died (in/on) a plane crash.

　　＜解答＞ in

1723. Let's sit (under/below) that apple tree.

　　＜解答＞ under

1724. (At/On) the top of the hill there were some cows grazing.

　　＜解答＞ At

1725. Many streets (in/at) the city need repairs.

　　＜解答＞ in

1726. Put the milk (in/into) the refrigerator.

　　＜解答＞ into

1727. There are several people (to wait/waiting) in line.

　　＜解答＞ waiting

1728. (Run/Running) ten miles a day is hard work.

　　＜解答＞ Running

1729. To sing well (take/takes) a lot of practice.

　　＜解答＞ takes

1730. A doctor's job is (to heal/healing) people.

　　＜解答＞ to heal

1731. Raising (their/his) hands, the pope blessed the crowd.

　　＜解答＞ his

1732. During the storm, the electricity (was knocked/knocked) out.

　　＜解答＞ was knocked

1733. How long (must/do must) we suffer ?

　　＜解答＞ must

1734. Bus service will resume (on/in) Friday morning.

　　＜解答＞ on

1735. The Simons put their house (up/on) for sale on Friday, and it was sold by Monday.

　　＜解答＞ up

1736. If you want good Szechuan cooking, (you/we) should go to the Hot Wok Restaurant.

　　＜解答＞ you

1737. Bob met Sally, who was in town for a few days, (and they/they) went to a museum.

　　＜解答＞ and they

1738. The old man sitting on the park bench is the father of a dozen men and women besides (to be/being) the grandfather of nearly forty children.

　　＜解答＞ being

1739. Conrad and Isabel got married, (they/and they) invited several friends to a party.

    ＜解答＞ and they

1740. Start attended college, (he/but he) left after a year.

    ＜解答＞ but he

1741. (After he/He) signed the treaty, President Lee asked the Senate to ratify it.

    ＜解答＞ After he

1742. Although they are expensive to install, solar heating systems save money and energy, (they/which) are hard to get these days.

    ＜解答＞ which

1743. (Because he/He) came from the planet Krypton, Superman had special powers that no one on Earth could equal, though many people have tried.

    ＜解答＞ because he

1744. After his store burned down, Mr. Crossman rented the store across the street, (his/and his) business continued to do well.

    ＜解答＞ and his

1745. Eric wanted to go to the new disco, which he had heard was a great place, (but he/he) did not want to see his ex-wife.

    ＜解答＞ but he

1746. Ann Landers (gives/give) advice to millions of Americans.

    ＜解答＞ gives

1747. Whoever (go/goes) to bed last should shut off the lights.

    ＜解答＞ goes

1748. Brushing (one's/your) teeth and getting checkups regularly are two important parts of good dental care.

    ＜解答＞ one's

1749. The child in this old photograph is (me/I).

    ＜解答＞ I

1750. The girl who loves Peter is (she/her).

    ＜解答＞ she

1751. David's new job seemed (what/that) he had hoped for.

<解答>　what

1752. (Give/To give) whoever calls today this information.

<解答>　Give

1753. The men (whom/who) you see are waiting for work.

<解答>　whom

1754. Hansen is the person to (whom/who) Wilmot gave the bribe money.

<解答>　whom

1755. The typewriter was stolen by the messenger about (whom/who) the office
manager had been suspicious.

<解答>　whom

1756. The dishes are not clean, so don't use (it/them).

<解答>　them

1757. The home team won (their/its) final game of the season.

<解答>　its

1758. The visiting team felt (they/it) deserved to win.

<解答>　they

1759. Almost anyone can earn a good living if (they/he or she) works hard.

<解答>　he or she

1760. Neither Earle nor Jeff could find (his/their) coat.

<解答>　his

1761. Show me (who/whom) is waiting to see me.

<解答>　who

1762. Discuss this form with (whoever/whomever) applies for the job.

<解答>　whoever

1763. (We/Us) women have responded to the challenge of the 1980's.

<解答>　We

1764. They are discriminating against (we/us) women.

<解答>　us

1765. (You/They) boys should play more quietly.

<解答> you

1766. (We/Us) Democrats support President Carter's bid for re-election.

<解答> We

1767. Mom sent (we/us) children to bed.

<解答> us

1768. Won't you give (us/we) boys a chance to earn some money ?

<解答> us

1769. Many Orientals were on the plane with (us/we) Americans.

<解答> us

1770. Paul's father wants (he/him) to help paint the house.

<解答> him

1771. Should Fred ask (she/her) to join the club ?

<解答> her

1772. Pat didn't expect my friend to be (he/him).

<解答> him

1773. My twin brother is often thought to be (I/me).

<解答> I

1774. (Their/They're) apartment costs a lot of money.

<解答> Their

1775. The woman (whose/who's) typewriter I borrowed, gave it to me.

<解答> who's

1776. Buba's (to shout/shouting) attracted a large crowd.

<解答> shouting

1777. My (being/to be) sick caused me to miss an important lecture.

<解答> being

1778. We, my brother and (I/me), are going hunting together.

<解答> I

1779. Uncle Joe gave us, Stuart and (me/I), tickets to the World Series.

<解答> me

1780. The money (having/has) been spent, the boys decided to go home.

<解答> having

1781. A minority in Congress (is/are) delaying passage of the bill.

<解答> is

1782. A minority of Congressmen (want/wants) to defeat the bill.

<解答> want

1783. The jury (has/have) asked for many times.

<解答> has

1784. The jury (are/is) unable to agree.

<解答> are

1785. Each of the candidates (want/wants) an opportunity to discuss his beliefs.

<解答> wants

1786. Anyone (is/are) allowed to use the public beach.

<解答> is

1787. Many of the drawings (were/was) beautiful.

<解答> were

1788. A few of the windows (were/was) broken.

<解答> were

1789. Several of Joe's friends (are/is) sorry that he left.

<解答> are

1790. Many a woman (feels/feel) entitled to more in life than just housework.

<解答> feels

1791. Every man, woman, and child (wanted/wants) to be happy.

<解答> wants

1792. Some of the books (have/has) been lost.

<解答> have

1793. Some of work (was/were) completed.

<解答> was

1794. All of the ice cream (is/are) gone.

<解答> is

1795. All of the men (have/has) left.

＜解答＞　have

1796. Most of the talk (was/were) about football.

＜解答＞　was

1797. Most of the people (were/was) dissatisfied.

＜解答＞　were

1798. Neither the mother nor her daughter (was/were) ever seen again.

＜解答＞　was

1799. One or the other of us (has/have) to buy the tickets.

＜解答＞　has

1800. Neither the plumber nor the painters (have/has) finished.

＜解答＞　have

1801. Either the branch officers or the main office (closes/close) at 4.

＜解答＞　closes

1802. She or you (are/is) responsible.

＜解答＞　are

1803. You or she (is/are) mistaken.

＜解答＞　is

1804. (Are/Is) the cat and the dog fighting ?

＜解答＞　Are

1805. Coming at us from the left (was/were) an ambulance.

＜解答＞　was

1806. There (are/is) two things you can do.

＜解答＞　are

1807. There (is/are) only one bottle left.

＜解答＞　is

1808. What (is/are) the name of your friend ?

＜解答＞　is

1809. What (are/is) the addresses of some good restaurants ?

＜解答＞　are

1810. Who (is/are) the man standing over there ?

<解答>　is

1811. Here (comes/come) my friend.

<解答>　comes

1812. Our biggest problem (is/are) angry customers.

<解答>　is

1813. More gas guzzlers (aren't/isn't) what this country needs.

<解答>　aren't

1814. The amount shown, plus interest, (is/are) due on Friday.

<解答>　is

1815. The president, together with his advisers (is/are) at Camp David.

<解答>　is

1816. He doesn't (has/have) two radios.

<解答>　have

1817. (Do/Does) most watches have two hands and a face.

<解答>　Do

1818. John always (open/opens) the windows for the teacher.

<解答>　opens

1819. Mr. Smith also (eats/eat) in the cafeteria everyday.

<解答>　eats

1820. The teacher also (carrys/carries) his books in a briefcase.

<解答>　carries

1821. Pedro and Henry also (play/plays) tennis every afternoon.

<解答>　play

1822. There (is/are) a magazine on the chair.

<解答>　is

1823. There (are/is) many English classes in our school.

<解答>　are

1824. There (isn't/aren't) many new words in this lesson.

<解答>　aren't

1825. (Are/Is) there several magazines on the table ?

　　　＜解答＞ Are

1826. (That/Those) pocketbook on the table belongs to Mary.

　　　＜解答＞ That

1827. There are two (churchs/churches) on this street.

　　　＜解答＞ churches

1828. (Tomatos/Tomatoes) are my favorite vegetable.

　　　＜解答＞ Tomatoes

1829. Marie always (trys/tries) to come to school on time.

　　　＜解答＞ tries

1830. I know both (he/him) and his brother very well.

　　　＜解答＞ him

1831. She says that she sees Karen and (he/him) on the bus every morning.

　　　＜解答＞ him

1832. I (bought/buyed) all my books in the school bookstore.

　　　＜解答＞ bought

1833. My father usually (gets/got) up early every morning.

　　　＜解答＞ gets

1834. They may (be not/not be) back before noon.

　　　＜解答＞ not be

1835. They (not/don't) go to the movies every night.

　　　＜解答＞ don't

1836. It (doesn't rain/don't rains) very often during the month of April.

　　　＜解答＞ doesn't rain

1837. Does he (read/reads) a lot of computer magazines ?

　　　＜解答＞ read

1838. There (wasn't/weren't) many new words in the lesson.

　　　＜解答＞ weren't

1839. Why (does/did) John walk to school alone every day ?

　　　＜解答＞ does

1840. (Do/Were) there many students absent from the lesson ?

<解答>　Were

1841. (Do/Did) Julio read about the accident in the newspaper last night ?

<解答>　Did

1842. There is a map on the wall just (on/above) the teacher's desk.

<解答>　above

1843. I was late (for/to) my lesson this morning.

<解答>　for

1844. She asked me all (about/of) my trip to Chicago.

<解答>　about

1845. At the end of the school year, I (selled/sold) all my books.

<解答>　sold

1846. We (not had/didn't have) a good time at the party last night.

<解答>　didn't have

1847. (Had they/Did they have) a very good time in Mexico last summer ?

<解答>　Did they have

1848. I saw (you/yours) on the bus this morning.

<解答>　you

1849. He always speaks to (us/our) in English.

<解答>　us

1850. It (will be/will is) very warm during this season of the year.

<解答>　will be

1851. The weather (willn't/won't) be warm tomorrow.

<解答>　won't

1852. (Will they/Do they will) travel to both France and England during the summer.

<解答>　Will they

1853. It was a (quick/quickly) lunch because they wanted to go shopping.

<解答>　quick

1854. I was sick for several weeks, but I am (good/well) now.

<解答>　well

1855. (No/Not) one girl wanted to dance with him.

<解答> Not

1856. There is (not/no) a really serious student in the whole class.

<解答> not

1857. The teacher (found/finded) many mistakes in our compositions.

<解答> found

1858. We walked (along/by) the river for about an hour.

<解答> along

1859. For the class picture, the tall students stood (near/behind) the short ones.

<解答> behind

1860. Look ! Janet (wave/is waving) to us from the other side of the street.

<解答> is waving

1861. Mr. And Mrs. Eng (are building/build) a new home on Second Street.

<解答> are building

1862. We always (have/are having) a good time at Helen's parties.

<解答> have

1863. (Is/Does) Mr. Berger taking his daughter with him on his trip.

<解答> Is

1864. Julia says that she (is/is going to be) a doctor when she grows up.

<解答> is going to be

1865. I always take (a/the) Seventh Avenue subway to my work.

<解答> the

1866. During a hard storm, the wind (blew/blowed) down some of our palm trees.

<解答> blew

1867. The wedding, (who/which) was held at the bride's home, was on June 22.

<解答> which

1868. The class, (which/who) meets only once a week, was canceled.

<解答> which

1869. The weather today is (more warm/warmer) than it was yesterday.

<解答> warmer

1870. Sue prepares her homework (carefullier/more carefully) than I do.

    ＜解答＞ more carefully

1871. August is the (hottest/most hot) month of the year in the United States.

    ＜解答＞ hottest

1872. I spoke to her (on/with) the telephone yesterday.

    ＜解答＞ on

1873. Ellen lives directly (across/on) the street from us.

    ＜解答＞ across

1874. He says that he saw (some/any) police officers on the corner.

    ＜解答＞ some

1875. Maybe you learned some, but I didn't learn (some/any).

    ＜解答＞ any

1876. However, she says that she doesn't have (some/any) famous clients.

    ＜解答＞ any

1877. She lives (somewhere/anywhere) on Sunset Boulevard.

    ＜解答＞ somewhere

1878. Now I can't find them (somewhere/anywhere).

    ＜解答＞ anywhere

1879. There wasn't (something/anything) wrong with it a few minutes ago when I used it.

    ＜解答＞ anything

1880. There isn't (somebody/anybody) who can help him now.

    ＜解答＞ anybody

1881. That other magazine, however, is (too/very) large to go into my desk drawer.

    ＜解答＞ too

1882. That chair is (very/too) heavy for Sue. She cannot pick it up.

    ＜解答＞ too

1883. It is a (too/very) heavy chair, but Nora is strong and can easily pick it up.

    ＜解答＞ very

1884. She placed the accent (on/in) the wrong syllable.

　　　＜解答＞ on

1885. I saw the president (in/on) television last night.

　　　＜解答＞ on

1886. The doctor gave me some medicine (to/for) my cough.

　　　＜解答＞ for

1887. The dog hurt (myself/itself) when it jumed over the fence.

　　　＜解答＞ itself

1888. She says that she (herself/himself) will return the book to yoy.

　　　＜解答＞ herself

1889. It is natural that George speaks German well because he (has spoken/spoke) it all his life.

　　　＜解答＞ has spoken

1890. She and I are good friends. In fact, we (were/have been) friends for more than ten years.

　　　＜解答＞ have been

1891. You can believe William because he always (tells/says) the truth.

　　　＜解答＞ tells

1892. Henry (told/said) yesterday that he liked the new teacher very much.

　　　＜解答＞ said

1893. The teacher gave (to use/us) some homework.

　　　＜解答＞ us

1894. How many new words do you look up (in/for) your distionary every day ?

　　　＜解答＞ in

1895. She copied her speech word (for/by) from the encyclopedia.

　　　＜解答＞ for

1896. Anne wants (me to go/that I go) with her to the movies tonight.

　　　＜解答＞ me to go

1897. The sun (was shining/shone) brightly when I got up this morning.

　　　＜解答＞ was shining

1898. The man (suffered/was suffering) greatly when the ambulance arrived.

　　＜解答＞ was suffering

1899. There is something wrong (with/on) this telephone.

　　＜解答＞ with

1900. What are your plans (for/on) the weekend ?

　　＜解答＞ for

1901. He should be more careful (about/to) his health.

　　＜解答＞ about

1902. She (has not/doestn't have) to spend more time on her homework.

　　＜解答＞doesn't have

1903. (Have I/Do I have) to sign my name at the botton of the page ?

　　＜解答＞ Do I have

1904. He (is working/has been working) in that same office ever since I first met him.

　　＜解答＞ has been working

1905. Clara has lived in that same house (for/since) many years.

　　＜解答＞ for

1906. She has never been the same (since/ago) he went away.

　　＜解答＞ since

1907. Mr. Pellie has been teaching English ever (for/since) he returned to the United States.

　　＜解答＞ since

1908. The police said that they (received/had received) several similar reports the same evening.

　　＜解答＞ had received

1909. We saw, as soon as we arrived home, that someone (had broken/broke) into the house.

　　＜解答＞ had broken

1910. We (must/had to) go to the hospital last night to see a friend who is sick.

　　＜解答＞ had to

1911. Barbara came (to/for) the books that you promised to lend her.

<解答>　for

1912. He is coming to the Unites States just (to/for) study English.

<解答>　to

1913. He (saw/was going to see) a doctor about the pain in his back, but suddenly the pain disappeared.

<解答>　was going to see

1914. The newspaper said that the weather today (will/would) be cold.

<解答>　would

1915. She said she (might/may) go with us to the movies tongiht.

<解答>　might

1916. She explained to me what the word (means/meant).

<解答>　meant

1917. John (entered/got) nito the automobile first, and then I followed him.

<解答>　got

1918. Mr. Smith drank so much wine that I thought he was going to (become drunk/drunk).

<解答>　become drunk

1919. The police officer ran (after/to) the thief but could not catch him.

<解答>　after

1920. Roger is mad (with/at) me because I won't go to the beach with him.

<解答>　at

1921. (Not/No) one student from our group attended the meeting.

<解答>　Not

1922. He asked me what (was my name/my name was).

<解答>　my name was

1923. Last night, while we (went/were going) to the movies, we met some old friends.

<解答>　were going

1924. He (may hold/may be held) by the police for several days.

　　＜解答＞　may be held

1925. Can all these books (brorrowed/be borrowed) from the library ?

　　＜解答＞　be borrowed

1926. The war (not followed/was not followed) by a serious economic depression.

　　＜解答＞　was not followed

1927. In general, it takes several years to learn (a/the) foreign language.

　　＜解答＞　a

1928. Naturally, I cannot speak English (same rapidly/as rapidly as) the teacher.

　　＜解答＞　as rapidly as

1929. Juan said that he hadn't seen (someone/anyone) in the room.

　　＜解答＞　anyone

1930. I was frightened because people (were running/ran) and screaming all around me.

　　＜解答＞　were running

1931. Columbus, when he died, did not realize that he (discovered/had discovered) a new continent.

　　＜解答＞　had discovered

1932. A scarecrow is supposed to drive birds away (off/from) the garden.

　　＜解答＞　from

1933. Our team was playing (against/on) the team from the next town.

　　＜解答＞　against

1934. He took the child (by/with) the hand an helped her to cross the street.

　　＜解答＞　by

1935. The buses are always crowed (at/in) this time of day.

　　＜解答＞　at

1936. The police refuse to let (someone/anyone) visit the prisoner.

　　＜解答＞　anyone

1937. They always (have/are having) their music lesson on Tuesday at this time.

　　＜解答＞　have

1938. She works much harder (as/than) the other students.

<解答> than

1939. It has (cost/costed) her a great deal of money to educate her five children.

<解答> cost

1940. The plane was (supposed/suppose) to leave last night at midnight, but bad weather delayed it.

<解答> supposed

1941. This building is supposed to (be open/open) to the public every day.

<解答> be open

1942. He (used/used to be) a teacher before he went into business.

<解答> used to be

1943. He has been your teacher for a long time, (has/hasn't) he ?

<解答> hasn't

1944. He is supposed to leave tomorrow, (isn't/doesn't) he ?

<解答> isn't

1945. You won't menting this to anyone, (will/do) you ?

<解答> will

1946. Steve and Tom have stopped (to speak/speaking) to each other.

<解答> speaking

1947. We would appreciate (to receive/receiving) your answer immediately.

<解答> receiving

1948. They will begin (to build/build) their new home soon.

<解答> to build

1949. She will continue (to work/work) in that same office until June.

<解答> to work

1950. The police are going to (question/questioning) everyone about the robbery.

<解答> question

1951. Each teacher received a (notice/noticing) of the change in examination dates.

<解答> notice

1952. It is a question (to/of) getting permission from the authorities.
<解答> of

1953. She said that, (under/at) the circumstances, she could do noting for us.
<解答> under

1954. You (ought not/not ought) to write your compositions in pencil.
<解答> ought not

1955. She should (have been/had) more careful in handling such things.
<解答> have been

1956. If the weather (will be/is) nice tomorrow, we will go to the beach.
<解答> is

1957. If you (have/will have) time tomorrow, we can go to the ball game.
<解答> have

1958. If the weather continues to be so cold, I (will have/have) to buy some warmer clothings.
<解答> will have

1959. If I get a good grade on my examination, my parents (be/will be) pleased.
<解答> will be

1960. If he (paid/has paid) more attention in class, he would pass the course.
<解答> paid

1961. If he (doesn't/didn't) waste so much time in class, he would make more progress.
<解答> didn't

1962. If she knew how to drive well, she (will have/would have) fewer accidents.
<解答> would have

1963. If I had a good book to read, I (would/will) stay at home tonight and read.
<解答> would

1964. If I (am/were) a millionaire, I would spend every winter in Miami.
<解答> were

1965. If she were more ambitious, she (will/would) not be content with such a low-paying job.

　　　　<解答>　would

1966. If the weather yesterday (had been/was) nice, we would have gone to the beach.

　　　　<解答>　had been

1967. If I (knew/had known) about this yesterday, I could have brought the money with me.

　　　　<解答>　had known

1968. If she had paid more attention in class, she (had done/would have done) better on her examination.

　　　　<解答>　would have done

1969. If I had known it was going to rain, I (had taken/would have taken) my umbrella.

　　　　<解答>　would have taken

1970. I wish I (had known/knew) that you were going to the beach yesterday.

　　　　<解答>　had known

1971. I wish the weather (were/was) warm so that we could go to the park.

　　　　<解答>　were

1972. When the weather (gets/will get) warmer, you can go swimming.

　　　　<解答>　gets

1973. The program won't begin until the president (arrives/will arrive).

　　　　<解答>　arrives

1974. Peter insisted (on/in) helping me with my homework.

　　　　<解答>　on

1975. Because of his dark hair and eyes, everyone always takes Sam (for/after) my brother.

　　　　<解答>　for

1976. During our telephone conversation, Pam became angry and hung up (at/on) me.

　　　　<解答>　on

1977. How long (do you study/have you studied) English ?

　　　　<解答>　do you study

1978. He is supposed to work tomorrow, and I (am, too/am to work).

<解答＞ am, too

1979. He would like to see the movie, and (so would I/I would like to).

<解答＞ so would I

1980. He was absent from the lesson, and (his sister was, too/his sister was).

<解答＞ his sister was, too

1981. She likes to watch television, and (so does her husband/so likes her husband).

<解答＞ so does her husband

1982. You can't blame me for that mistake, and George can't, (either/neither).

<解答＞ either

1983. I didn't remember his name, and Henry (didn't, either/did, neither).

<解答＞ didn't, either

1984. He didn't have any money with him, and (neither/either) did I.

<解答＞ neither

1985. You won't enjoy that show, and (neither will your wife/your wife will neither).

<解答＞ neither will your wife

1986. At first, I didn't like living in New York, but now I (do/like).

<解答＞ do

1987. She says she knows him well, but I don't think she (knows/does).

<解答＞ does

1988. It is an hour (knew/to have known) such a distinguished woman.

<解答＞ to have known

1989. She is said (to have been/been) the strongest preson in the government.

<解答＞ to have been

1990. Gail must (have left/leave) home during the morning because she was not there when I telephoned at noon.

<解答＞ have left

1991. I imagine, from things they have told me, that they must (have been/be) very wealthy at one time.

<解答＞ have been

1992. It's strange Joe is not here for his appointment, but he may (forget/have forgotten) all about it.

　　＜解答＞　have forgotten

1993. They may (be/have been) wealthy at one time, but I doubt it.

　　＜解答＞　have been

1994. There (weren't/won't) many students absent from class today.

　　＜解答＞　weren't

1995. I will (be waiting/wait) for you on the corner at the usual time tomorrow morning.

　　＜解答＞　be waiting

1996. Tomorrow afternoon at this time, we will be (flying/fly) over the Caribbean Sea.

　　＜解答＞　flying

1997. He (had worked/worked) there for just a week when the accident happened.

　　＜解答＞　had worked

1998. When the police stopped the car, they asked the driver if he (had been drinking/had drunk).

　　＜解答＞　had been drinking

1999. Nobody thought the elevator was dangerous because they (had been going/went) up and down in it safely for years.

　　＜解答＞　had been going

2000. By the time Carlos leaves New York, he (will have done/will do) many interesting things.

　　＜解答＞　will have done

2001. She says that before she leaves, she (ate/will have eaten) at every restaurant in town.

　　＜解答＞　will have eaten

2002. Your telegram came just as I (left/was leaving) my house.

　　＜解答＞　was leaving

2003. When we got home, we discovered that Rose (had left/was leaving) a message on our machine.

<解答>　had left

2004. Sophie seemed pleased with the results of our examination, (didn't/wasn't) he ?

<解答>　didn't

2005. He couldn't understand a single word I said, (couldn't/could) he ?

<解答>　could

2006. She seems (have/to be having) trouble with that problem.

<解答>　to be having

2007. The output of the plant is said (is/to have been) a million tons a year.

<解答>　to have heen

2008. The nurse made us (to eake/take) the medicine.

<解答>　take

2009. Everyone heard them (to laugh/laugh).

<解答>　laugh

2010 The building across the street (is tearing/is being torn) down.

<解答>　is being torn

2011. Many new buildings in Caracas (were being constructed/were constructing) when I was there.

<解答>　were being constructed

2012. The mattress may (be delivered/deliver) while you're out.

<解答>　be delivered

2013. The other bills must (pay/be paid) by the end of the month.

<解答>　be paid

2014. He said that he (will/would) wait for us on the corner.

<解答>　would

2015. He told me that they (were crossing/are crossing) a field at the time.

<解答>　were crossing

2016. Her mother said she always (remembers/remembered) the important things.

<解答>　remembered

2017. My doctor (said/told) him to take two aspirin and plenty of vitamin C.
　　 ＜解答＞ told

2018. (What/How) a bright young lady her oldest daughter is !
　　 ＜解答＞ What

2019. (How/What) quickly they have learned English.
　　 ＜解答＞ How

2020. We don't make much money, but we (do/so) have a lot of fun.
　　 ＜解答＞ do

2021. It was Cortez who conquered Mexico, wasn't it ? I believe (too/so).
　　 ＜解答＞ so

2022. Perhaps he will give us the money. I don't think (so/either).
　　 ＜解答＞ so

2023. Mr. Lee has made good progress so far. Indeed (he has/has he) !
　　 ＜解答＞ he has

2024. They'll win first prize easily. Naturally (they will/will they) !
　　 ＜解答＞ they will

2025. I'm doing better work now, don't you agree ? of course (you are/are you) !
　　 ＜解答＞ you are

2026. I (used to/am used to) have a large breakfast every morning.
　　 ＜解答＞ used to

2027. He (used to/is used to) having his hair cut by the same barber.
　　 ＜解答＞ is used to

2028. However, we'd better not (gave/give) them too many details.
　　 ＜解答＞ give

2029. They'd better (to save/save) a little money for a change.
　　 ＜解答＞ save

2030. Dan prefers (to do/do) all his homework before he leaves school.
　　 ＜解答＞ to do

2031. We (had/would) rather spend the summer at home instead of in the country.
　　 ＜解答＞ would

2032. They (fell/felt) that they could talk to you in confidence.

<解答> felt

2033. If by chance the electricity (should/would) go off, we will have to work in the dark.

<解答> should

2034. If by chance a police officer should (see/ seeing) you driving that way, you'll get a ticket.

<解答> see

2035. (Lie/Lay) on this sofa for a few minutes until you feel stronger.

<解答> Lie

2036. Although he had (laid/lay) a cloth on the floor, the floor got stained.

<解答> laid

2037. The papers had been (lying/laying) in the rain for several hours.

<解答> lying

2038. He has been (laying/lying) here asleep since two o'clock.

<解答> lying

2039. The soldiers, (been/being) forced to march, pretended to be ill.

<解答> being

2040. (Left/Leaving) the party, we ran into Joyce and Tom.

<解答> Leaving

2041. I dislike (to go/going) away from home for long periods of time.

<解答> going

2042. Despite (the fact that/the fact) it was cold, we went to the ball game.

<解答> the fact that

2043. (In spite of/Despite of) the good advice we gave them, they didn't win the prize.

<解答> In spite of

2044. We took pictures of almost everything, but the (one/ones) we took of the bullfight turned out best.

<解答> ones

2045. My family went (as far as/until) Los Angeles on their vacation.

　　　＜解答＞　as far as

2046. She told me to stay in bed (until/as far as) I felt stronger.

　　　＜解答＞　until

2047. I won't see you, (as far as/until) I can tell, for some times.

　　　＜解答＞　as far as

2048. Try not to come (until/as far as) I have had my shower.

　　　＜解答＞　until

2049. Do they (still/anymore) have that crazy dog that barks at everyone constantly ?

　　　＜解答＞　still

2050. We are still good friends, although I don't see them very often (anymore/still).

　　　＜解答＞　anymore

2051. They have never sold that merchandise (anywhere else/else).

　　　＜解答＞　anywhere else

2052. Let's do (something/something else) tonight besides watch television.

　　　＜解答＞　something else

2053. (Whoever/Who) studies English always has difficulty with the pronunciation.

　　　＜解答＞　Whoever

2054. You can take whichever one you want, and you can bring it back

　　　(when/whenever) you wish.

　　　＜解答＞　whenever

2055. (What/Whatever) she cooks always turn out to have the same taste.

　　　＜解答＞　Whatever

2056. Janie spends too (little/few) time on her homework.

　　　＜解答＞　little

2057. We haven't heard (much/many) news lately.

　　　＜解答＞　much

2058. How (much/many) time do you have to spend with us ?

　　　＜解答＞　much

2059. There is (many/a lot of) grass in that meadow.

　　　＜解答＞　a lot of

2060. The thing they were (arguing about/arguing) was really of little importance.

　　　＜解答＞　arguing about

2061. She is the kind of representative it is difficult to get (away/away from).

　　　＜解答＞　away from

2062. The man claimed that someone had (stolen/robbed) him.

　　　＜解答＞　robbed

2063. This coffee seems (some/somewhat) better than usual.

　　　＜解答＞　somewhat

2064. The coffee was (some/somewhat) bitter.

　　　＜解答＞　somewhat

2065. Nowhere (you could/could you) find a more generous person.

　　　＜解答＞　could you

2066. Dennis carefully (spilled/poured) the cream into the pitcher.

　　　＜解答＞　poured

2067. The Port of London laid (embargo/embargoes) on all ships coming from the Baltic.

　　　＜解答＞　embargoes

2068. Blackmail is a (species/specie) of crime which we all hate.

　　　＜解答＞　species

2069. The (students parents/students' parents) were invited to the graduation.

　　　＜解答＞　students' parents

2070. It has always been this (newspapers policy/newspapers' policy) to report the news honestly and accurately.

　　　＜解答＞　newspapers' policy

2071. The two most common (metals/metal) for kitchen untensils are aluminum and stainless steel.

　　　＜解答＞　metals

2072. His (succeed/success) in business was the result of hard work.

<解答> success

2073. The (omit/omission) of a few words in the contract caused a great deal of trouble.

<解答> omission

2074. Although he was a word-renowned scientist, he always behaved with (humbleness/humble).

<解答> humbleness

2075. The police taking measures to prevent the (recur/recurrence) of any violence by the strikers.

<解答> recurrence

2076. They expressed their (indignant/indignation) by sending a lengthy petition to the mayor.

<解答> indignation

2077. The camper decided that the next time he would take along nothing that would be such a (hinder/hindrance) to him.

<解答> hindrance

2078. An overuse of slang words (mark/marks) a person as uneducated.

<解答> marks

2079. The number of people who understand Einstein's theory of relativity (is/are) very small.

<解答> is

2080. A number of people (are/is) waiting at the airport to greet the movie star.

<解答> are

2081. A second series of books on American literature (is/are) being planned by the publisher.

<解答> is

2082. His ethics in that business deal (is/are) being questioned by some financial experts.

<解答> are

2083. The Scotch (have/has) the reputation of being thrifty.

　　＜解答＞　have

2084. The seriously wounded (was/were) immediately taken to the hospital.

　　＜解答＞　were

2085. In (who/whose) house will the meeting be held ?

　　＜解答＞　whose

2086. The man (whose/ which) car was stolen went to the police immediately.

　　＜解答＞　whose

2087. Some students (of hers/of her) were on a TV discussion program.

　　＜解答＞　of hers

2088. That car (theirs/of theirs) always gave them trouble.

　　＜解答＞　of theirs

2089. The teachers tried to guess (who/whom) might be appointed as the new principal.

　　＜解答＞　who

2090. You should always depend on (you/yourself) rather than on someone else.

　　＜解答＞　yourself

2091. The party members (they/themselves) don't believe that their leaders are honest.

　　＜解答＞　themselves

2092. This package must be given to the president (itself/himself).

　　＜解答＞　himself

2093. The student must be made to understand how each lesson can be value to (them/him).

　　＜解答＞　him

2094. One should always be careful when (one/you) is crossing the street.

　　＜解答＞　one

2095. (They/You) never really know what love is until you experience it yourself.

　　＜解答＞　You

2096. Give this to one of the boys, (whichever/that) one comes to the door first.

<解答> whichever

2097. (Whoever/What) gave you permission to leave the office early ?

<解答> Whoever

2098. (Whatever/Who) happened to those nice people who used to live next door to you ?

<解答> Whatever

2099. Neither of the girls (has/have) done her homework.

<解答> has

2100. Each of the boy scouts is bringing (his/their) own camping equipment.

<解答> his

2101. All of the boy scouts (is/are) bringing their own camping equipment.

<解答> are

2102. Some of the machinery (need/needs) to be repaired.

<解答> needs

2103. All of the information on the report (are/is) correct.

<解答> is

2104. Most of the merchandise (have/has) sold.

<解答> has

2105. Half of the turkey (is/are) for today's dinner.

<解答> is

2106. (They/There) are three reasons for rejecting that proposal.

<解答> There

2107. (It/They) would be wise if you went there now.

<解答> It

2108. There (are/is) many simple recipes in this cookbook.

<解答> are

2109. To take a drive in the country (is/are) very pleasant.

<解答> is

2110. (That he/He) should resent such a remark is natural.

　　＜解答＞　That he

2111. It is becoming apparent (that/which) we will never finish on time.

　　＜解答＞　that

2112. I (prophesy/prophecy) that the world would be destroyed in the year 2000.

　　＜解答＞　prophesy

2113. The watch has already been (winded/wound) today.

　　＜解答＞　wound

2114. The dictator is such a typant that many people have (fleed/fled) from the country.

　　＜解答＞　fled

2115. She (tasted/is tasting) the soup to see if it needs more salt.

　　＜解答＞　is tasting

2116. Just as he reached the bus stop, the bus (passes/passed) by him.

　　＜解答＞　passed

2117. He (is working/was working) in a restaurant the last time I saw him.

　　＜解答＞　was working

2118. She was washing the dishes when the phone (rings/rang).

　　＜解答＞　rang

2119. (While they/They) were watching television the lights went out.

　　＜解答＞　While they

2120. (Just as/Just) we were sitting down to dinner, our uncle came.

　　＜解答＞　Just as

2121. The travel agency (will planning/will be planning) our itinerary.

　　＜解答＞　will be planning

2122. He still has not realized what a bad mistake he (made/has made.).

　　＜解答＞　has made

2123. They (have just spent/have just been spending) three weeks at their country home.

　　＜解答＞　have just spent

2124. A plane heades for the West Cost (crashed/has crahes) in the mountains last night.

    ＜解答＞　crashed

2125. Before his mother (has said/had said) one word of reprimand, the child began to cry.

    ＜解答＞　had said

2126. Because she had not reported the theft immediately, the police (were/had been) unable to help her.

    ＜解答＞　were

2127. They never received the books which they (had ordered/has ordered).

    ＜解答＞　had ordered

2128. We (had just sat/just had sat) down to dinner when a fire broke out in kitchen.

    ＜解答＞　had just sat

2129. He (had scarcely begun/scarcely had begun) to work on his new job when he became seriously ill with pneumonia.

    ＜解答＞　had scarcely begun

2130. They had no sooner sold their car (than/when) they regretted having done so.

    ＜解答＞　than

2131. The actor who (has been playing/had been playing) the part of Hamlet became too ill to go to on stage.

    ＜解答＞　had been playing

2132. He (had never missed/had never been missing) a day's performance until he became ill.

    ＜解答＞　had never missed

2133. At he end of this summer, I (shall have been/shall have) away from home for ten years.

    ＜解答＞　shall have been

2134. When he retires from his work, he (will make/will have made) more than a million dollars.

    ＜解答＞　will have made

2135. The car (had just been/had just) bought by the young couple when it was stolen by some teen-agers.

<解答> had just been

2136. The money (shouldn't been left/shouldn't be left) in cash register at night.

<解答> shouldn't be left

2137. Car owners (haven't been warned/haven't warned) to lock their cars.

<解答> haven't been warned

2138. The plan will be landing soon, (won't it/doesn't it) ?

<解答> won't it

2139. He hasn't been having financial trouble, has he ? No, he (hasn't/has).

<解答> hasn't

2140. The old house burned down, didn't it ? Yes, it (did/didn't).

<解答> did

2141. They couldn't have left the office early, (could/couldn't) they ?

<解答> could

2142. Might he (be stopped/stopped) if he tries to cross the border ?

<解答> be stopped

2143. She (must have been/must have) in a great hurry to leave for the theater because she left all the dinner dishes on the table.

<解答> must have been

2144. He may have (stolen/been stealing) for a long time without his parents knowing about it.

<解答> been stealing

2145. For all we know, the child may have (been abandoned/abandoned) by its mother some time ago.

<解答> been abandoned

2146. The money would (sent/have been sent) to you it once if we had known your address.

<解答> have been sent

2147. When I was a boy, I (could able to/was able to) speak several foreign languages.

　　＜解答＞ was able to

2148. This error (can corrected/can be corrected) easily.

　　＜解答＞ can be corrected

2149. You (may/might) borrow my car if you drive carefully.

　　＜解答＞ may

2150. In those days, anyone (may/might) enroll for the course.

　　＜解答＞ might

2151. John's mother said that he (can/could) go with us.

　　＜解答＞ could

2152. She (should to eat/should eat) less if she wants to lose weight.

　　＜解答＞ should eat

2153. Everyone (ought to go/ought) to the dentist once a year.

　　＜解答＞ ought to go

2154. Mr. Johnson ought (to have/to have gone) to the dentist yesterday, but he was too busy.

　　＜解答＞ to have gone

2155. You (don't have to/not have to) pay in person; you can pay by check.

　　＜解答＞ don't have to

2156. (Most/Do) we have to write a thesis in order to get a degree ?

　　＜解答＞ Do

2157. I don't know what's the matter. The train (should been/should have been) here an hour ago.

　　＜解答＞ should have been

2158. We ordered the books months ago. They (should arrive/should have arrived) long before now.

　　＜解答＞ should have arrived

2159. One of my classmates looks quite depressed. He not (pass/have passed) the examination.

<解答> have passed

2160. His credit card was mailed a week ago. He (should receive/should have received) it by now.

<解答> should have received

2161. I would rather (wear/have worn) a fur coat than a cloth coat last winter.

<解答> have worn

2162. The Browns would rather have gone to the movies (than/than to) the theater.

<解答> than to

2163. We often serve dinner outdoors, and so (that/do) our neighbors.

<解答> do

2164. The owner of the factory worked just as hard as his employees (did/do) in order to get the order out on time.

<解答> did

2165. The children were placed in (every other/other every) seat for the examination.

<解答> every other

2166. He had (many too/too many) other places to visit to stay there long.

<解答> too many

2167. He claims he needs some more money; however, he has (much more/more much) money than he will admit.

<解答> much more

2168. She earns much (little/less) money than her husband does.

<解答> less

2169. If he ever gets out of his country he will try to live in (free/ the freest) land in the world.

<解答> the freest

2170. Student groups all over the world are becoming more (rebel/rebellious) against autority.

<解答> rebellious

2171. After the heavy rains the roads became so (mud/muddy) that they couldn't be used.

<解答>　muddy

2172. She has always behaved in a (duty/dutiful) way toward her parents.

　　　<解答>　dutiful

2173. His recent religious conversion has made him so (piety/pious) that he is forever praying and fasting.

　　　<解答>　pious

2174. He is very (hesitate/hesitant) about taking such a long trip.

　　　<解答>　hesitant

2175. Even late at night you can find (few/a few) people still working at their desks.

　　　<解答>　a few

2176. Not (anyone/someone) can do this work; it requires intelligence and speed.

　　　<解答>　anyone

2177. He refused to take (any/some) compencation for the work he had done.

　　　<解答>　any

2178. The coat you just bought is (like/alike) the one I bought last year.

　　　<解答>　like

2179. Mother and daughter were (alike/like) in their fear of snakes.

　　　<解答>　alike

2180. (The/A) smoke coming from the forest fire can be seen for miles around.

　　　<解答>　The

2181. (A/The) newspaper is one of the most widespread media of communication.

　　　<解答>　The

2182. (An/A) engineer must have a good knowledge of mathematics and physics.

　　　<解答>　An

2183. (The/An) imprisonment of people without a trial is not part of the democratic process.

　　　<解答>The

2184. (Himalayas/The Himalayas) have been referred to as " the roof of the world. "

　　　<解答>　The Himalayas

2185. Tea is grown in many parts of (the southern/southern) Asia, especially in India and Ceylon.

<解答> southern

2186. Don't worry so much about the future; it's (the present/present) that is most important.

<解答> the present

2187. The later we get to the theater, (the/a) worse seats will get.

<解答> the

2188. The more work we do now, the (little/less) we'll have to do later.

<解答> less

2189. The (high/higher) prices rose, the more money the workers asked for.

<解答> higher

2190. They are men who (know/knows) what they want.

<解答> know

2191. (What/What a) useless information they are gathering.

<解答> What

2192. This car has (such a/such) powerful motor.

<解答> such a

2193. For the hedonist, (a pleasure/pleasure) is considered the greatest good.

<解答> pleasure

2194. She told the doctor she had (a pain/pain) in her back.

<解答> a pain

2195. I have been looking forward to (meet/meeting) you.

<解答> meeting

2196. We wouldn't mind (to wait/waiting) your friends.

<解答> waiting

2197. Someone had broken into the office and (stole/stolen) the files.

<解答> stolen

2198. Having eaten and (drank/drunk) too much the night before, he woke up with a headache.

<解答>　drunk

2199. The rug needs (cleaned/cleaning) before we move in.

<解答>　cleaning

2200. The hem of this dress needs (mended/to be mended) before I wear it again.

<解答>　to be mended

2201. I don't know (how/that) to use the card catalog in the library.

<解答>　how

2202. Until he came to the United States to study, he didn't know (to cook/how to cook).

<解答>　how to cook

2203. I (used to study/was used to studying) at the University of Southern California before I transferred here.

<解答>　was used to studying

2204. We (use to/used to) go to the movies quite frequently.

<解答>　used to

2205. The light is always out in her room at ten o'clock; she (must have/must) go to bed early every night.

<解答>　must

2206. This pen won't write; it (can/must) have run out of ink.

<解答>　must

2207. We had better (make/made) reservations so that we will be sure of getting a good table.

<解答>　make

2208. You had better (don't quit/not quit) your job until you find another one.

<解答>　not quit

2209. (Won't/Would) you like to go swimming with us tomorrow ?

<解答>　Would

2210. (Do/Would) you like to have dinner with us tonight ?

<解答>　Would

2211. She told me that she'd rather not (serve/to serve) on the committee.

<解答> serve

2212. He said that he'd rather (went/go) to a small college instead of to a large university.

<解答> go

2213. He had hoped that he (graduate/would graduate) this semester, but he couldn't finish his thesis in time.

<解答> would graduate

2214. His father had hoped that he (would go/go) into business with him.

<解答> would go

2215. If you (would go/went) to bed earlier, you wouldn't be so sleepy in the morning.

<解答> went

2216. If we (finish/finished) our work a little early today, we'll attend the lecture at the art museum.

<解答> finish

2217. I wish that the snow (will/would) stop soon.

<解答> would

2218. Mary wishes that she (has studied/had studied) law instead of history when she was in college.

<解答> had studied

2219. Mary wishes that she (could have studied/studied) law instead of history when she was in college.

<解答> could have studied

2220. Mary wishes that she (could study/would have studied) law instead of history when she was in college.

<解答> would have studied

2221. Bill wishes that she (is/were) more interested in his work.

<解答> were

2222. If it (is/were) not so far, we could go for the weekend.

<解答> were

2223. He complied with the requirement that all graduate students in education (should write/write) a thesis.

<解答> write

2224. The foreign student advisor recommended that she (studied/study) more English before enrolling at the university.

<解答> study

2225. It is not necessary that you (must take/take) an entrance examination to be admitted to an American university.

<解答> take

2226. It is essential that all applications and transcripts (are/be) filed no later than July 1.

<解答> be

2227. Professor Baker let us (to write/write) a paper instead of taking a final exam.

<解答> write

2228. Have you had your temperature (taking/taken) yet ?

<解答>taken

2229. She understood the question, (didn't/wasn't) she ?

<解答> didn't

2230. You can buy almost anything in a drug store, (can't/couldn't) you ?

<解答> can't

2231. He's writing her another letter, (isn't/hasn't) he ?

<解答> isn't

2232. We'd decided to open a joint account, (couldn't/hadn't) we ?

<解答> hadn't

2233. We are going to the concert, and (so do they/so are they).

<解答> so are they

2234. I am worried about it, and (also is he/so is he) .

<解答> so is he

2235. She hasn't finished the assignment yet, and (neither I have/neither have I).

＜解答＞ neither have I

2236. He won't be here today, and (either his sister will/his sister won't either).

＜解答＞ his sister won't either

2237. Would you please (don't smoke/not smoke).

＜解答＞ not smoke

2238. Would you please (not to be late/not be late).

＜解答＞ not be late

2239. If your brother (invited/were invited), he would come.

＜解答＞ were invited

2240. References (not used/are not used) in the examination room.

＜解答＞ are not used

2241. The party is a surprise but all of her friends (coming/are coming).

＜解答＞ are coming

2242. I can't talk with you right now because the doorbell (is ringing/reinging).

＜解答＞ is ringing

2243. In my opinion, (it is too/too) soon to make a decision.

＜解答＞ it is too

2244. The book that I lent you (has a/a) good bibliography.

＜解答＞ has a

2245. In the entire history of the solar system, thirty billion planets may (has/have) been lost or destroyed.

＜解答＞ have

2246. It is essential that nitrogen (is/be) present in the soil for plants to grow.

＜解答＞ be

2247. If the eucalyptus tree (were/was) to become extinct, the koala bear would also die.

＜解答＞ were

2248. Some teachers argue that student who (are used to/used to) using a calculator may forget how to do mental calculations.

　　＜解答＞　are used to

2249. A new automobile needs (to tuned/to be tuned) up after the first five thousand miles.

　　＜解答＞　to be tuned

2250. Light rays can make the desert (appears/appear) to be a lake.

　　＜解答＞　appear

2251. Do you really believe that she has blamed us for the accident, especially (you and I/you and me) ?

　　＜解答＞　you and me

2252. When he comes back from vacation, (Bob and me/Bob and I) plan to look for another apartment.

　　＜解答＞　Bob and I

2253. The experiment proved to my lab partner and (me/I) that prejudices about the result of an investigation are often unfounded.

　　＜解答＞　me

2254. The cake is from Jan and the flowers are from Larry and (we/us).

　　＜解答＞　us

2255. I would appreciate (you letting/your letting) me know as soon as possible.

　　＜解答＞　your letting

2256. He is surprised by (your having/you having) to pay for the accident.

　　＜解答＞　your having

2257. Did you meet the girl (whom/who) was chosen Honecoming Queen ?

　　＜解答＞　who

2258. There is often disagreement as to (who/whom) is the better student, Bob or Ellen.

　　＜解答＞　who

2259. There is someone on line two (which/who) would like to speak with you.

　　＜解答＞　who

2260. The student (who/which) receives the highest score will be awarded a scholarship.

<解答>　who

2261. A child can usually feed (self/himself) by the age of six months.

<解答>　himself

2262. An oven that cleans (its/itself) is very handy.

<解答>　itself

2263. It is considered cheating when students help (each the other one/each other) on tests or quizzes.

<解答>　each other

2264. They will never find (each another/each other) at this crowded airport.

<解答>　each other

2265. Officials at a college or university must see a student's transcripts and financial guarantees prior to (them/their) issuing him or her a form I-20.

<解答>　their

2266. It was (she/her), Ann Sullivan, who stayed with Helen Keller for fifty years, teaching and encouraging her student.

<解答>　she

2267. Most foreign students realize that it is important for (themselves/them) to buy health insurance while they are living in the United States, because hospital costs are very high.

<解答>　them

2268. When an acid and a base neutralize (one the other/one another), the hydrogen from the acid and the oxygen from the base join to form water.

<解答>　one another

2269. Through elected officials, a representative democracy includes citizens like you and (I/me) in the decision-making process.

<解答>　me

2270. She bought a small (amount/number) of tickets.

<解答>　number

2271. There are only (a few/few) seats left.

<解答>　a few

2272. (A/A piece of) mail travels faster when the zip code is indicated on the envelope.

　　＜解答＞ A piece of

2273. (Each/Each piece of) furniture in this display is on sale for half price.

　　＜解答＞ Each piece of

2274. We saw several (kind/kinds) of birds at the wildlife preserve.

　　＜解答＞ kinds

2275. I only know how to run (one type of/one type a) computer program.

　　＜解答＞ one type of

2276. Flight 606 for Los Angeles is now ready of boarding at (the concourse seven/concourse seven).

　　＜解答＞ the concourse seven

2277. Look in (volume second/volume two) of the Modern Medical Dictionary.

　　＜解答＞ volume two

2278. (Winning prizes/Winning of prizes) is not as important as playing well.

　　＜解答＞ Winning prizes

2279. (Direct/The direct) dialing of overseas numbers is now common.

　　＜解答＞ The direct

2280. The ptarmigan, like a large (number/amount) of Arctic animals, is white in winter and brown in summer.

　　＜解答＞ number

2281. (Art/The art) of colonial America was very functional, consisting mainly of useful objects such as furniture and household utensils.

　　＜解答＞ The art

2282. (Dam/A dam) is a wall constructed across a valley to enclose an area in which water is stored.

　　＜解答＞ A dam

2283. (The stare/To stare) at a computer screen for long periods of time can cause severe eyestrain.

　　＜解答＞ To stare

2284. All (business' students/business students) must take the Graduate Management Admission Test.

＜解答＞ business students

2285. I forgot their (telephone's number/telephone number).

＜解答＞ telephone number

2286. A (three-minute/three-minutes) call anywhere in the United States cost less than a dollar when you dial it yourself.

＜解答＞ three-minute

2287. I have to write a (one-thousand-word/one thousand-words) paper this weekend.

＜解答＞ one-thousand-word

2288. We have (not a file/no file) under the name Wang.

＜解答＞ no file

2289. Bill told me that he has (none/no) friends.

＜解答＞ no

2290. Drug abuse is increasing at an (alarmed/alarming) rate.

＜解答＞ alarming

2291. The petition has been signed by (concerning/concerned) citizens.

＜解答＞ concerned

2292. This suitcase is (so/as) heavy that I can hardly carry it.

＜解答＞ so

2293. Preparing frozen foods is (too/so) easy that anyone can do it.

＜解答＞ so

2294. We had (such/so) a small lunch that I am hungry already.

＜解答＞ such

2295. That so many advances have been made in (so short/so short a) time is the most valid argument for retaining the research unit.

＜解答＞ so short a

2296. He always plays his stereo (so/too) loud.

＜解答＞ too

2297. It is too cold (go/to go) swimming.

<解答> to go

2298. He should be (as strong enough/strong enough) to get out of bed in a few days.

<解答> strong enough

2299. His score on the exam was (enough good/good enough) to qualify him for a graduate program.

<解答> good enough

2300. (For play/To play) golf well, don't move your feet when you swing.

<解答> To play

2301. Virginia always boils the water twice (make/to make) tea.

<解答> to make

2302. Although the medicine tastes (bad/badly), it seems to help my condition.

<解答> bad

2303. The music sounds (sweet/sweetly) and soothing.

<解答> sweet

2304. After only six months in the United States, Jack understood everyone (perfect/perfectly).

<解答> perfectly

2305. Passengers travel (comfortable/comfortably) and safely in the new jumbo jets.

<解答> comfortably

2306. Although he ran as (fastly/fast) as he could, he did not win the race.

<解答> fast

2307. When students register (lately/late) for classes, they must pay an additional fee.

<解答> late

2308. She has been living here (before/since) April.

<解答> since

2309. We haven't seen him (since/for) almost a year.

<解答> for

2310. School starts on (sixteen/the sixteenth of) September this year.

<解答> the sixteenth of

2311. Please change my reservation to (the ten of/the tenth of) November.
　　＜解答＞　the tenth of

2312. Most of us are sponsored (from/by) our parents.
　　＜解答＞　by

2313. One problem is finding an apartment, another is furnishing it, and (other/the other) is getting the utilities turned on.
　　＜解答＞　the other

2314. Some of these T-shirts are red, (another/others) are blue, and the rest are white.
　　＜解答＞　others

2315. The orchid family includes more (than/that) seven thousand species.
　　＜解答＞　than

2316. Humorist Will Rogers was brought up on a cattle ranch in the Oklahoma Indian territory, but the life of a cowboy was not (excited/exciting) enough for him.
　　＜解答＞　exciting

2317. The age of a body of water may be determined (for/by) meassuring its tritium content.
　　＜解答＞　by

2318. Red corpuscles are so numerous that a thimbleful of (human's/human) blood would contain almost ten thousand million of them.
　　＜解答＞　human

2319. Is you book the same (to/as) mine ?
　　＜解答＞　as

2320. My briefcase is exactly (the same that/like) yours.
　　＜解答＞　like

2321. We didn't buy the car because they wanted (as much twice as/twice as much as) it was worth.
　　＜解答＞　twice as much as

2322. Her qualifications are (better than/better than those) of any other candidate.
　　＜解答＞　better than those

2323. The audience is much (larger than/larger than that at) last year's concert.

<解答> larger than that at

2324. The more you study during the semester, (the less/the lesser) you have to study the week before exams.

<解答> the less

2325. The oxygen concentration in the lungs is (higher than/higher than that of) the blood.

<解答> higher than that of

2326. There is a disagreement among industrialists as to whether the products of this decade are (inferior to/inferior those of) the past.

<解答> inferion those of

2327. According to the coroner, she died not of injuries sustained in the accident, (only/but) of a herat attack.

<解答> but

2328. You can put everything (but/but for) those silk blouses in the washer.

<解答> but

2329. The mail comes at ten o'clock every day (except/not) Saturday.

<解答> except

2330. It is important to eat well at lunchtime (instead of/in place) buying snacks from vending machines.

<解答> instead of

2331. By using coupons, you can get a discount on a lot of things, (such/such as) groceries, toiletries, and household items.

<解答> such as

2332. Did they tell you (what time the movie started/what time does the movie start)?

<解答> what time the movie started

2333. Every student needs a social security number (so/so that) he can get a university identification card made.

<解答> so that

2334. Classes will be canceled tomorrow (because/because of) a national holiday.

    ＜解答＞ because of

2335. It was difficult to see the road clearly (because/because of) it was raining.

    ＜解答＞ because

2336. It is an accepted custom for a man to open the door when he (accompanies/accompanied) a woman.

    ＜解答＞ accompanies

2337. Mr. Davis tries to finish his research, but he (found/finds) only part of the information which he needs.

    ＜解答＞ finds

2338. Professor Baker told his class that the best way to understand the culture of another country (is/was) to live in that country.

    ＜解答＞ was

2339. When she told us that everything (is/was) ready, we went into the dining room and seated ourselves.

    ＜解答＞ was

2340. Although there (are/were) only two hundred foreign students studying at State University in 1970, there are more than five hundred now.

    ＜解答＞ were

2341. Before he died, the man who (lives/lived) across the street used to help me with my English.

    ＜解答＞ lived

2342. Just before he died, my friend who (writes/wrote) poetry published his first book.

    ＜解答＞ wrote

2343. Before the 1920s, no women (had/will have) voted in the United States.

    ＜解答＞ had

2344. Styles that (have been/were) popular in the 1940s have recently reappeared in high-fashion boutiques.

    ＜解答＞ were

2345. The chestnut tree used to be an important species in the Eastern forests of the United States until a blight (killed/kills) a large number of trees.
    ＜解答＞ killed

2346. All trade between the two countries (was/were) suspended pending negotiation of a new agreement.
    ＜解答＞ was

2347. The production of different kinds of artificial materials (are/is) essential to the conservation of our natural resources.
    ＜解答＞ is

2348. Mary, accompanied by her brother on the piano, (were/was) very well received at the talent show.
    ＜解答＞ was

2349. Never again (they will stay/will they stay) in that hotel.
    ＜解答＞ will they stay

2350. Very seldom (can a movie hold/a movie can hold) my attention like this one.
    ＜解答＞ can a movie hold

2351. The first two problems are very difficult, but the rest (is/are) easy.
    ＜解答＞ are

2352. Four miles (have/has) been recorded on the odometer.
    ＜解答＞ has

2353. Those of us who are over fifty years old should get (our/their) blood pressure checked regularly.
    ＜解答＞ our

2354. Although their visas will expire in June, they can have (it/them) extended for three months.
    ＜解答＞ them

2355. Whoever called did not leave (his/their) name number.
    ＜解答＞ his

2356. In order to graduate, one must present (their/one's) thesis days prior to the last day of classes.

<解答> one's

2357. The ozone layer, eight to thirty miles above the earth, (protects/protect) us from too many ultraviolet rays.

<解答> protects

2358. It is believed that dodo birds forgot how to fly and eventually became extinct because there (were/was) no natural enemies on the isolated island of Masarine where they lived.

<解答> were

2359. Accustomed to getting up early, (A. he had no difficulty adjusting to the new schedule./B. the new schedule was not difficult for him to adjust to.)

<解答> A

2360. While finishing his speech, (A. the audience was invited to ask question./B. he invited the audience to ask questions.)

<解答> B

2361. We learned to read the passages carefully and (to underline/underlining) the main ideas.

<解答> to underline

2362. The patient's symptoms were fever, dizziness, and (his head hurt/headaches).

<解答> headaches

2363. Flying is not only faster but also (it is safer/safer) than traveling by car.

<解答> safer

2364. The three thousand stars visible to the naked eye can be seen because they are either extremely bright (or they are/or) relatively close to the earth.

<解答> or

2365. To apply a passport, fill out the application form, attach two recent photographs, and (take/taking) it to your local office or passport office.

<解答> take

2366. A person who purchases a gun for protection is six times more likely to kill a friend or relative than (killing/to kill) an intruder.

<解答> to kill

2367. (A. That she has known him for a long time influenced her decision./B. That it is she has known him for a long time influenced her decision.)

＜解答＞ A

2368. Mary had always behaved (in a responsible manner/responsibly).

＜解答＞ responsibly

2369. Bill asked the speaker (to repeat/to repeat again) because he had not heard him the first time.

＜解答＞ to repeat

2370. She (returned back/returned) to her hometown after she had finished her degree.

＜解答＞ returned

2371. My teacher (he said/said) to listen to the news on the radio in order to practice listening comprehension.

＜解答＞ said

2372. My sister (found/she found) a store that imported food from our country.

＜解答＞ found

2373. One hundred thousand earthquakes are felt every year, one thousand of which cause (severe serious/severe) damage.

＜解答＞ severe

2374. The corporation, which is by far the most influential form of business ownership, is a comparatively new (innovation/organization).

＜解答＞ organization

2375. The longest mountain range, the Mid Atlantic Range, is (not hardly/hardly) visible because most of it lies under the ocean.

＜解答＞ hardly

2376. One of the magnificent Seven Wonders of the Ancient World was the (enormous large/enormous) statue known was the Colossus of Rhodes.

＜解答＞ enormous

2377. Limestone formations growing downward from the roofs of (caves/caves that they) are stalactites.

<解答> caves

2378. The most common name in the world (it is/is) Mohammad.

<解答> is

2379. That comets' tail are caused by solar wind (is generally accepted/generally accepted).

<解答> is generally accepted

2380. Irving Berlin, America's most prolific songwriter, (he never/never) learned to read or write music.

<解答> never

2381. That the earth and the moon formed (simultaneously at the same time/simultaneously) is a theory that accounts for the heat of the early atmosphere surrounding the earth.

<解答> simultaneously

2382. The Navajo language was used (in a successful manner/successfully) as a code by the United States in World War II.

<解答> successfully

2383. It is the first digit that appears on any zip code that (it refers/refers) to one of ten geographical areas in the United States.

<解答> refers

2384. The cost of living (has raised/has risen) over 8 percent in the past year.

<解答> has risen

2385. Margaret (told/said) that she would call before she came.

<解答> said

2386. Stan had an accident while he was driving the car that his cousin had (lent/borrowed) him.

<解答> lent

2387. Professor Baker wouldn't (let/leave) us use our dictionaries during the test.

<解答> let

2388. (Except for/Excepting for) the Gulf Coast region, most of the nation will have very pleasant weather tonight and tomorrow.

<解答> Except for

2389. It is interesting to compare the customs of other countries (to/with) those of the United States.

<解答> with

2390. Even young children begin to show (able/ability) in mathematics.

<解答> ability

2391. The (develop/development) of hybrids has increased yields.

<解答> development

2392. The (manage/management) of small business requires either education or experience in sales and accounting.

<解答> management

2393. Occasionally dolphins need (to rise/to raise) to the surface of the water to take in oxygen.

<解答> to rise

2394. Ice has the same (hard/hardness) as concrete.

<解答> hardness

2395. Terrorists are capable (to/of) hijacking planes and taking hostages in spite of security at international airports.

<解答> of

2396. Some business analysts argue that the American automobile industry is suffering because Congress will not impose heavier import duties, but others say that the care themselves are (inferior to/inferior with) the foreign competition.

<解答> inferior to

2397. When a human being gets hurt, the brain excretes a chemical called enkaphalin to numb the (pain/painful).

<解答> pain

2398. Thomas Jefferson's home, which he designed and built, (sits/sets) on a hill overlooking the Weshington, D.C., area.

<解答> sits

2399. It is not the TOEFL but the academic preparation of a student that is the best indicator of his (success/successfully).

　　＜解答＞ success

2400. The brand-new car is (theirs/their); it has many desirable features, such as automatic overdrive and a rear-window defroster.

　　＜解答＞ theirs

2401. I was sleepy, and I longed for my (comfortable/comfortably) bed.

　　＜解答＞ comfortable

2402. The coach blew the whistle, (and/but) the runners began the race.

　　＜解答＞ and

2403. Industries in the community (has/have) suffered in recent years.

　　＜解答＞ have

2404. However, their search for leftovers (create/creates) problems for Kodiak.

　　＜解答＞ creates

2405. A desk and a bookcase (was/were) moved into my younger brother's bedroom.

　　＜解答＞ were

2406. The sailboats in the harbor (belong/belongs) to the village.

　　＜解答＞ belong

2407. Mrs. Shea or her father (sweep/sweeps) their front path every day.

　　＜解答＞ sweeps

2408. The fate of the players (depend/depends) on the coach's instruction.

　　＜解答＞ depends

2409. (There's/There are) a pint of strawberries in the kitchen.

　　＜解答＞ There's

2410. The stuffed animals in my collection (sit/sits) on a shelf in my closet.

　　＜解答＞ sit

2411. Several paintings by that artist (are/is) on exhibit at the mall.

　　＜解答＞ are

2412. The hot-water pipes in the laundry room have (bursted/burst) again.

　　＜解答＞ burst

2413. How many sixth-graders have never (rode/ridden) on the school bus ?

　　　＜解答＞ ridden

2414. In Alice's Adventures in Wonderland, Alice (shrank/shrunk) to a very small size.

　　　＜解答＞ shrank

2415. Are you and (they/them) going to the besketabll game ?

　　　＜解答＞ they

2416. Mr. Lee divided the money among the younger children and (they/them).

　　　＜解答＞ them

2417. In the skit, when Pygmalion returned from the festival of Venus, (him/he) and the statue were supposed to hug.

　　　＜解答＞ he

2418. That was Carl and (they/them) in the swimming pool.

　　　＜解答＞ they

2419. Finally, the judges announce that the winners of the safety contest are (us/we) Ramblers.

　　　＜解答＞ we

2420. Of all the days in the week, Friday goes by (more slowly/most slowly).

　　　＜解答＞ most slowly

2421. One by one, they felt the contents of the mystery bag (cautious/cautiously).

　　　＜解答＞ cautiously

2422. Although the slip was sinking, the loyal crew would not (desert/dessert) the captain.

　　　＜解答＞ desert

2423. Which of these two boxes of (stationary/stationery) do you like better ?

　　　＜解答＞ stationery

2424. The man who'd been hired to (lead/led) the wagon train planned to rob its people and desert them.

　　　＜解答＞ lead

2425. The police found a briefcase full of (counterfeit/copied) money in the car.

<解答>　counterfeit

2426. It is (doubtful/suspicious) that I will win the national spelling competition.

<解答>　doubtful

2427. Those oily rage in the corner of the basement are a fire (risk/hazard).

<解答>　hazard

2428. That diet is dangerous, (for/but) it does not meet the body's needs.

<解答>　for

2429. Those two students are twins, (yet/or) they do not dress alike.

<解答>　yet

2430. (As we/We) were walking home, we stopped to watch a game.

<解答>　As we

2431. (Although both/Both) teams played their best, only one could be the winner.

<解答>　Although both

2432. The students may type their reports, (or/but) they may write them neatly.

<解答>　or

2433. To the east of our school is the community center, (and/but) to the west is the fire station.

<解答>　and

2434. A network of warning signals (alert/alerts) people in coastal areas of an approaching tidal wave.

<解答>　alerts

2435. My guide and companion on the tour (was/were) Pilar.

<解答>　was

2436. A horse and buggy (was/were) once a fashionable way to travel.

<解答>　was

2437. At the press conference, there (was/were) several candidates for mayor and two for governor.

<解答>　were

2438. The Veterans of Foreign Wars (is/are) holding its convention in our city this year.
＜解答＞ is

2439. Both (he and she/her and him) have promised to write us this summer.
＜解答＞ he and she

2440. Orange juice tastes (more sweetly/sweeter) than grapefruit juice.
＜解答＞ sweeter

2441. When we came into the house after ice-skating, the fire felt (good/well).
＜解答＞ good

2442. I read in the newspaper (where/that) the President enjoys horseback riding.
＜解答＞ that

2443. It was warm this morning, (so I/I) left my jacket at home.
＜解答＞ I

2444. Do you know (how come/why) the library is closed today.
＜解答＞ why

2445. My complaint was that the sandwiches we took to the beach were (three fourths/three-fourths) sand.
＜解答＞ three-fourths

2446. " Can you volunteer just two (hours/hours') worth of your time a week ?
＜解答＞ hours'

2447. The snow has melted everywhere (accept/except) in the mountains.
＜解答＞ except

2448. She was happy to (accept/except) the invitation to the school dance.
＜解答＞ accept

2449. A bicyclist can wear out a set of (brakes/breaks) going down a steep mountain.
＜解答＞ brakes

2450. You should use soft (cloths/clothes) to clean silver.
＜解答＞ cloths

2451. A nation may (brake/break) a treaty that no longer serves its interests.
＜解答＞ break

2452. The city council will not meet unless seven of the ten (councilors/counselors) are present.

<解答>　councilors

2453. The patient received (council/counsel) from the doctor on the best course to a speedy, safe recovery.

<解答>　counsel

2454. Mustard and relish are the usual (complements/compliments) of hot dogs.

<解答>　complements

2455. Our camp (councilor/counselor) advised us to eat fruit for our dessert.

<解答>　counselor

2456. I want your counsel, not your (complements/compliments).

<解答>　compliments

2457. That noise is from a jet plane going (threw/through) the sound barrier.

<解答>　through

2458. A moving target is harder to hit (than/then) a stationary one.

<解答>　than

2459. The pilot has to decide (weather/whether) to parachute to safety or try to land the crippled plane.

<解答>　whether

2460. The girls' basketabll team not only won the game (and/but also) scored the most points in our school's history.

<解答>but also

2461. I didn't receive a letter from my cousin today, (nor/or) did I really expect one.

<解答>　nor

2462. Members of the aduience sometimes use stage ashtrays, (or/and) they hang their coats on the actors' coat racks.

<解答>　or

2463. (After we/We) have written our report on the history of computers, we may be able to go to the picnie.

<解答>　After we

2464. (While the/The) stage crew was constructing the sets, the performers continued their rehearsal.

<解答> While the

2465. Both of Fred's brothers (celebrates/celebrate) their birthdays in July.

<解答> celebrate

2466. Most of the appetizers on the restaurant menu (tastes/taste) delicious.

<解答> taste

2467. Our guava tree and our fig tree (bears/bear) more fruits than our entire neighborhood can eat.

<解答> bear

2468. Either the students or the teacher (reads/read) aloud during the last ten minutes of each class period.

<解答> reads

2469. Neither the seal nor the clowns (catches/catch) the ball that the monkey throws into the circus ring.

<解答> catch

2470. Some of the tourists foolishly (approches/approach) the wild bears to give them food.

<解答> approach

2471. The public (differs/differ) in their opinions on the referendum.

<解答> differ

2472. The trees lost several of (their/its) branches in the thunderstorm last night.

<解答> their

2473. Each of these magazines has had the President's picture on (its/his) cover.

<解答> its

2474. One of my uncles always wears (his/their) belt buckle off to one side.

<解答> his

2475. No person should be made to feel that (he/it) is worth less than someone else.

<解答> he

2476. The fire engine and the police car went rushing by with (their/its) lights flashing.

＜解答＞ their

2477. Nearly every one of the girls in our class had (their/her) hair cut short.

＜解答＞ her

2478. Every one of the soldiers carried extra rations in (their/his) pack.

＜解答＞ his

2479. All of the volunteers quickly went to work at (his or her/their) job.

＜解答＞ their

2480. A person should weigh (their/his) words carefully before criticizing someone else.

＜解答＞ his

2481. The club often (argues/argue) among themselves about finances and activities.

＜解答＞ argue

2482. My spelling lessons and acience homework sometimes (takes/take) me hours to finish.

＜解答＞ takes

2483. In most cases, a dog or a cat that gets lost in the woods can take care of (themselves/itself).

＜解答＞ itself

2484. I don't understand how chameleons sitting on a green leaf or a bush change (their/its) color.

＜解答＞ their

2485. Please ask some of these girls to pick up (her/their) own materials from the supply room.

＜解答＞ their

2486. The air conditioner and the refrigerator have switches that turn (it/them) off and on automatically.

＜解答＞ them

2487. The audience clapped (their/its) hands in approval.

　　＜解答＞　their

2488. The referee is (sitting/setting) the ball on the fifty-yard line.

　　＜解答＞　setting

2489. Luckily, it was not (them/they) in the accident.

　　＜解答＞　they

2490. It might have been (him/he), but I'm not sure.

　　＜解答＞　he

2491. If the singer had been (her/she), I would have listened.

　　＜解答＞　she

2492. The film editor showed the visitors and (we/us) students around the television station.

　　＜解答＞　us

2493. Please invite your cousin and (they/them) to the horse show this Saturday.

　　＜解答＞　them

2494. I wrote a story about my great-grandmother and (he/him).

　　＜解答＞　him

2495. We should try to learn from (passed/past) experience.

　　＜解答＞　past

2496. We were (shone/shown) all the points of interest in the downtown area.

　　＜解答＞　shown

2497. Our (invincible/victorious) army never has been and never should be defeated in battle.

　　＜解答＞　invincible

2498. Medieval artists had a special (fashion/technique) for making stained-glass windows.

　　＜解答＞　technique

2499. Although the lawyer stayed within the law, he relied on (guile/fraud) to win his case.

　　＜解答＞　guile

2500. Computer science, in addition to foreign languages, (are/is) offered at our junior high school.

<解答> is

2501. Romeo and Juliet (are/is) required reading in our English class, and many of the students are eager to begin this play.

<解答> is

2502. The brook between the two hills (are/is) filled with trout.

<解答> is

2503. Geraldo knows what to expect at camp, but Ines (don't/doesn't) have any idea.

<解答> doesn't

2504. I can't read Steven's poem because there (is/are) too many smudges on the paper.

<解答> are

2505. Few of the people here for vacation (wants/want) to live here year-round.

<解答> want

2506. The confusion among shoppers (is/are) certainly understandable.

<解答> is

2507. For example, the quantity printed on yogurt containers (tells/tell) the number of ounces in a container.

<解答> tell

2508. Different brands of juice (shows/show) the same quantity in different ways.

<解答> show

2509. Shoppers, confusion, along with rising prices, (is/are) a matter of concern to consumer groups.

<解答> is

2510. The units in this system (has/have) a relationship to one another.

<解答> have

2511. The traditional system of indicating quantities (makes/make) shopping a guessing game.

<解答> makes

2512. A shopper on the lookout for bargains (does not/do not) know whether liquid or solid measure is indicated.

<解答> does not

2513. One can with a label showing twenty-four ounces (contains/contain) the same quantity as a can with a label showing one pint eight ounces.

<解答> contains

2514. The metric system, in use in European countries, (solves/solve) most of the confusion.

<解答> solves

2515. Consumer groups in this country (continues/continue) to advocate a uniform system of measurement.

<解答> continue

2516. Three quarters of the movie (was/were) over when we arrived.

<解答> was

2517. Two thirds of the missing books (was/were) returned.

<解答> were

2518. Mathematics (is/are) an important part of many everyday activities.

<解答> is

2519. Four weeks (is/are) enough time to rehearse the play.

<解答> is

2520. Taxes (is/are) always a main issue during an election year.

<解答> are

2521. Not one of the ushers (knows/know) where the lounge is.

<解答> knows

2522. Carol, as well as Irene, (writes/write) a column for the East High Record.

<解答> writes

2523. " Beauty and the Beast " (is/are) a folk tabe that exists in many different cultures.

<解答> is

2524. It is difficult to concentrate when there (is/are) radios and stereos blasting away.

<解答> are

2525. In most situation comedies, there (is/are) very wise characters, very foolish characters, and very lovable characters.

<解答> are

2526. Ten pounds (is/are) far too much weight for a young child to carry in a backpack.

<解答> is

2527. (Has/Have) either of you read To Kill a Mockingbird.

<解答> Has

2528. Someone else in our class has also submitted (their/his) topic.

<解答> his

2529. Dominic, one of the Perrone twins, has chosen Alfred Hitchcock as (their/his) subject.

<解答> his

2530. Does everyone, including George and Dominic, know that (they/she) must assemble facts, not opinions ?

<解答> she

2531. Many a sailor (have/has) perished on this coast, crashing on its partly submerged rocks.

<解答> has

2532. When the truck overturned, a herd of cattle (were/was) set free on the expressway.

<解答> was

2533. Richard, along with many others, (don't/doesn't) always concentrate hard enough on math problems.

<解答> doesn't

2534. Measles (have/has) been almost completely conquered by a vaccine.

<解答> has

2535. In a short time, we had surprised (she/her) and several bystanders with our ability.

<解答> her

2536. That author (who/whom) you admire is scheduled to visit the local bookstore next Tuesday.

<解答> whom

2537. It was John Adams (who/whom) founded the American Society of Arts and Letters.

<解答> who

2538. Her grandmother, to (who/whom) she sent the flowers, won the over-fifty marathon.

<解答> whom

2539. sometimes it was difficult to tell who was having a better time, (them or us/they or we).

<解答> they or we

2540. During the Olympic trials, every diver except (she/her) received a low score from the judges.

<解答> her

2541. My schedule this year includes English, social studies, science, (etc./and etc.)

<解答> etc.

2542. Did you (bring/take) flowers to your aunt when you visited her in her new home ?

<解答> take

2543. Perhaps I should (of/have) called before coming to see you at your home.

<解答> have

2544. Perhaps the young couple (hadn't ought/ought not) to have married at all.

<解答> ought not

2545. On the news, I heard (where/that) the game was called off because of rain.

<解答> that

2546. He would not have released the report (without/unless) he had first verified his sources.

<解答>　unless

2547. I (haven't/have) borrowed but one book from the library this week.

<解答>　have

2548. You will be pleased to hear, Sumi, that two poems of (yours/yours') have been selected for the literary magazine.

<解答>　yours

2549. It wasn't (anyone's/anyones') fault that we missed the bus.

<解答>　anyone's

2550. (Eithers/Either's) project may win first prize at the Science Fair.

<解答>　Either's

2551. (One's/Ones') teeth should be checked regularly.

<解答>　One's

2552. (Everybodys'/Everybody's) trees must be irrigated.

<解答>　Everybody's

2553. Melissa knows how to use a (plain/plane) in shop class.

<解答>　plane

2554. Do you think your coffee (plain/plane) or with milk ?

<解答>　plain

2555. Norrine enjoys playing the French horn. Unfortunately, (on the other hand/however), she has no place where she can practice without disturbing others.

<解答>　however

2556. Many adults discover talenta that they never knew they had. Mother's cousin Ralph, (as a result/for example), became an accomplished metal sculptor in his fifties.

<解答>　for example

2557. Kerri and Mitch were wearing their seat belts when a driver crashed into the rear of their car. (As a result/Finally), they were not injured badly, although their car was totaled.

　　＜解答＞　As a result

2558. (Because/Although) human beings have no gills, they cannot stay underwater for long periods of time without special breathing equipment.

　　＜解答＞　Because

2559. No one wearing street shoes is allowed to enter the Norikami Museum. If you wish to enter, (therefore/on the other hand), you must leave your shoes outside and wear paper slippers.

　　＜解答＞　therefore

2560. Ruth mowed the lawn (while we/we) weeded the flower beds.

　　＜解答＞　while we

2561. The grass looked (it/as if it) had not been cut in months.

　　＜解答＞　as if it

2562. (Because the/the) house had been empty for so long, the lawn and gardens were choked with weeds.

　　＜解答＞　Because the

2563. We borrowed tools (so that we/we) could weed more efficiently.

　　＜解答＞　so that we

2564. (Until we/We) had pulled out the weeds, we could not see the roses.

　　＜解答＞　Until we

2565. (After Ruth/Ruth) had mowed about half the lawn, she was exhausted.

　　＜解答＞　After Ruth

2566. (When we/We) stopped for a rest, we stretched out in the shade.

　　＜解答＞　When we

2567. Long hours in the hot sun had made us feel (as though the day/the day) would never end.

　　＜解答＞　as though the day

2568. The jury (has/have) been paying close attention to the evidence in this case.

　　＜解答＞　has

2569. It (doesn't/don't) seem right to read letters addressed to someone else.
　　＜解答＞ doesn't

2570. Disregard for the rights and comforts of others (is/are) rude.
　　＜解答＞ is

2571. The members of the family (meets/meet) for a reunion every year.
　　＜解答＞ meet

2572. The carpeting in the upstairs and downstairs rooms (is/are) worn.
　　＜解答＞ is

2573. The package of radio parts (was/were) smahed in the mail.
　　＜解答＞ was

2574. The cost of two new snow tires (was/were) more than I expected.
　　＜解答＞ was

2575. The three boxes of dried mint (fits/fit) easily on the bottom shelf.
　　＜解答＞ fit

2576. The escape of three snakes from the laboratory (has/have) created quite a stir.
　　＜解答＞ has

2577. In the movie, a ring of dancers (performs/perform) a folk dance.
　　＜解答＞ performs

2578. The community college course on collecting stamps and coins (attracts/attract) many people.
　　＜解答＞ attracts

2579. That big tree with the oddly shaped leaves (seems/seen) to be dying.
　　＜解答＞ seems

2580. The chief, along with two of the firefighters, (gives/give) lectures on home safety.
　　＜解答＞ gives

2581. Participation in class discussions, not just high test scores, (counts/count) toward one's final grade.
　　＜解答＞ counts

2582. Could it be that nobody among all the world's animal loves (wants/want) to take these puppies off my hands ?

　　＜解答＞　wants

2583. If anyone comes in now, (he/they) will see what a mess we've made.

　　　＜解答＞　he

2584. There (is/are) leftover macaroni and cheese on the top shelf in the refrigerator.

　　　＜解答＞　is

2585. A philosopher once said that if someone built a better mousetrap, the world would beat a path to (his/their) door.

　　　＜解答＞　his

2586. There (was/were) women, as well as men, who set out on the perilous journey into new territory.

　　　＜解答＞　were

2587. About half the dog owners at the dog show (was/ were) complaining about the judges' incompetence and threatening to remove.

　　　＜解答＞　were

2588. Francis said that in a few years he would give his stamp collection to his brother and (I/me).

　　　＜解答＞　me

2589. Everyone was waiting impatiently to find out (who/whom) the new cheerleader would be.

　　　＜解答＞　who

2590. After he had spoken at the assembly, the senator agreed to meet with our class president and (we/us).

　　　＜解答＞　us

2591. She is one of those people (who/whom) can analyze oppnents' moves quickly.

　　　＜解答＞　who

2592. We found that it was (she/her) who called twice while were out of town.

　　　＜解答＞　she

2593. She is the teacher (who/whom) will coach the varsity golf team this year.

　　　＜解答＞　who

2594. As the runners approached the finish line, we saw Lisle and (he/him) break
ahead of the others.
＜解答＞ him

2595. Although her grandfather was the person for (who/whom) the town was named,
she moved away immediately after graduation.
＜解答＞ whom

2596. I need to know today if you and (she/her) plan to go with us on the trip.
＜解答＞ she

2597. I am going to vote for (whoever/whomever) can present the best solution to
environmental problems.
＜解答＞ whoever

2598. My little sister is a much better chess player than (I/me).
＜解答＞ I

2599. After the bake sale, give the remaining cookies and cakes to everyone
(who/whom) worked.
＜解答＞ who

2600. Before the debate started, I noticed that my opponent was as nervous as (I/me).
＜解答＞ I

2601. The teacher said that (whoever/whomever) was ready could give a speech first.
＜解答＞ whoever

2602. Seeing a car with an out-of-state license plate in my driveway, I ran inside, and
(who/whom) do you think was there ?
＜解答＞ who

2603. Please give my message to (whoever/whomever) answers the phone.
＜解答＞ whoever

2604. For (who/whom) is this criticism instended ?
＜解答＞ whom

2605. The duke directed a haughty sneer at the jester and (he/him).
＜解答＞ him

2606. Nobody understood the problem but Kevin and (he/him).

<解答> him

2607. In 1969 the governor needed a secretary of labor (on whom/who) he could depend.

<解答> on whom

2608. The person (who/whom) he appointed would occupy the most difficult and sensitive position in the cabinet.

<解答> whom

2609. She praised her compatriots, (whom/from whom) new advancess in agricultive had recently come.

<解答> from whom

2610. I think that the people who were costumed as pirates as (they/them).

<解答> they

2611. The author, (who/whom) the critices had praised, autographed a copy of his novel for me.

<解答> whom

2612. The teacher gave the assignment to (whomever/whoever) was absent yesterday.

<解答> whoever

2613. Can you run the two hundred meters as fast as (them/they) ?

<解答> they

2614. The sleet whirled about George and (he/him) until they could barely see.

<解答> him

2615. My sister (came/come) into my room to remind me to clean up the mess in the kitchen.

<解答> came

2616. I dived off the high board and (swam/swum) the length of the pool.

<解答> swam

2617. The clothing had (lain/laid) streun about the room all week.

<解答> lain

2618. (Lying/Laying) the tip by my plate, I rose to leave the restaurant.

＜解答＞ Laying

2619. Thomas as (sitting/setting) out the appetizers for the party guests.

＜解答＞ setting

2620. She (sat/set) down at her desk with her checkbook and calculator in front of her.

＜解答＞ sat

2621. John took over the reins of government and ruled in the (disagreeablest/most disagreeable) manner his subjects had known.

＜解答＞ most disagreeable

2622. After Diego had started lifting weights, he bragged that he was stronger than (any other man/any man) in town.

＜解答＞ any other man

2623. Why does that ketchup always come out of the bottle so (slow/slowly) ?

＜解答＞ slowly

2624. In the Northern Hemisphere, days in June are warmer (than/than days in) November.

＜解答＞ than days in

2625. Finding that the new map as (usefuller/more useful) to me than old one, I took it with me in the car.

＜解答＞ more useful

2626. A. Sitting on the telephone wire, he saw a meadowlark./B. He saw a meadowlark sitting on the telephone wire.

＜解答＞ B

2627. Looking through the telescope, (I thought the/the) moon seemed enormous.

＜解答＞ I thought the

2628. (While out running/While he was out running), his mouth got dry.

＜解答＞ While he was out running

2629. (As we were going/Going) around the bend, the ocean came into view.

＜解答＞ As we were going

2630. (While I was doing/Doing) a few tap dance steps, the floor got scratched.

<解答> While I was doing

2631. A. We watched the mother cat carefully cleaning her whiskers.

B. Carefully cleaning her whiskers, we watched the mother cat.

<解答> A

2632. A. To grow plants successfully, light, temperature, and humidity must be carefully controlled./B. To grow plants successfully, one must carefully control light, temperature, and humidity.

<解答> B

2633. (After doing/After we had done) the housework, the room almost sparkled.

<解答> After we had done

2634. A. To make manicotti, pasta must be stuffed with cheese.

B. To make manicotti, you must stuff pasta with cheese.

<解答> B

2635. A. When the lawyer had finished her speech, the jury looked at her in awe.

B. Concluding her speech, the jury looked at her in awe.

<解答> A

2636. My sister's statement (implied/ inferred) that she was displeased with the cut in her allowane.

<解答> implied

2637. From his letter I (implied/inferred) he would be away all summer.

<解答> inferred

2638. (Emigration/Immigration) to Alaska was spurred by the gold rush.

<解答> Immigration

2639. The heat has affected the growing season; we'll harvest (fewer/less) cropa this year.

<解答> fewer

2640. Was it George Washington Carver or Thomas Edison who (invented/discovered) all those uses for peanuts ?

<解答> discovered

2641. Many French Canadians (emigrated/immigrated) from Quebec to work in the industries of New England.

＜解答＞ emigrated

2642. Mary Beth Stearns (discovered/invented) a device to study electrons.

＜解答＞ invented

2643. This is a powerful machine, so treat it (respectfully/respectively).

＜解答＞ respectfully

2644. We went to the hardware store for a special (sort of/sort of a) wrench.

＜解答＞ sort of

2645. Adelita stayed (inside/inside of) the building until the rain stopped.

＜解答＞ inside

2646. John was trying in vain to (learn/teach) me some new dance steps.

＜解答＞ teach

2647. You can do (like/as) you like, but you should do as you think best.

＜解答＞ as

2648. The muskrat slipped (off/of) the bank smoothly and swam away.

＜解答＞ off

2649. Why did she feel (like/as if) she'd said something wrong ?

＜解答＞ as if

2650. We should mind our own business and (leave/let) that porcupine mind his.

＜解答＞ let

2651. We didn't want to take the boat out because the waves looked (sort of/rather) choppy.

＜解答＞ rather

2652. A solar eclipse (is/occurs) when the moon comes between the earth and the sun.

＜解答＞ occurs

2653. I found the right equipment in the catalog and ordered (same/it).

＜解答＞ it

2654. A run-on sentence (is where/means that) two sentences are erroneously joined as one.

　　＜解答＞ means that

2655. (Them/These) mosquitoes can drive a person nearly crazy.

　　＜解答＞ These

2656. Betty heard on the radio (where/that) the mayor is going to Washington about.

　　＜解答＞ that

2657. I'm tired of trying to cut the grass with (this here/this) old lawn mower that should be in an antique exhibit.

　　＜解答＞ this

2658. I see (where/that) pandas are an endangered species.

　　＜解答＞ that

2659. We (hadn't ought/ought not) to decide until we know more facts.

　　＜解答＞ ought not

2660. San Diego is quite a (way/ways) from here, but we ought to get there by 4:00.

　　＜解答＞ way

2661. We don't live in that neighborhood (no more/any more).

　　＜解答＞ any more

2662. She doesn't know (nothing/anything) about football, and she doesn't like it.

　　＜解答＞ anything

2663. We might have gone on the tour, but we wouldn't have had (no/a) camera to take pictures.

　　＜解答＞ a

2664. Since there (wasn't scarcely/was scarcely) any rain last spring, there are fewer mosquitoes this summer.

　　＜解答＞ was scarcely

2665. I saw on the news (where/that) manufacturers will start putting thoses air bags into all the new cars.

　　＜解答＞ that

2666. (Leave/Let) us work a while longer on the motor; we can't leave it this way.

<解答>　Let

2667. Would you like to be the first student to ride in a (Space Shuttle/space shuttle) that orbits the earth ?

<解答>　space shuttle

2668. That novel takes place in the Middle (Ages/ages) and highlights the problems of the feudal system.

<解答>　Ages

2669. I know (you're/your) upset with the plan, but it's the only way to solve the problem.

<解答>　you're

2670. Jack's achievement test scores ranked in the (eighty eighth/eighty-eighth) percentile.

<解答>　eighty-eighth

2671. The general spoke to the troops to improve their (moral/morale).

<解答>　morale

2672. The three kinds of blood vessels are arteries, veins, and (caterpillars/capillaries).

<解答>　capillaries

2673. A (liter/litter) is a nest of young baby animals.

<解答>　litter

2674. The earth makes a (revolution/resolution) every twenty-four hours.

<解答>　revolution

2675. Many young women are now joining the Marine (corpse/Corps).

<解答>　Corps

2676. It is well known that a (diseased/deceased) body can affect the mind.

<解答>　diseased

2677. The dodo is a bird that is totally (distinct/extinct) now.

<解答>　extinct

2678. A (maggot/magnet) is a worm you find in a bad apple.

　　＜解答＞ maggot

2679. Geometry teaches us to bisect (angels/angles).

　　＜解答＞ angles

2680. When you haven't got enough iodine in your blood, you get a (goiter/garter).

　　＜解答＞ goiter

2681. To collect the gases, hold a (baker/beaker) over the flame.

　　＜解答＞ baker

2682. Smoking cigarettes in bed (is/are) the cause of many tragic fires.

　　＜解答＞ is

2683. Many who give their time to help the disabled (works/work) as volumteers at the Special Olympics.

　　＜解答＞ work

2684. Bob Beamon's record long jump in the 1968 Olympics (stands/stand) as an achievement some people believe will never be matched.

　　＜解答＞ stands

2685. Basketabll, like many other games, (offers/offer) enjoyment and exercise to all who participate.

　　＜解答＞ offers

2686. When I begin cutting out this skirt pattern, I know I'll discover that my scissors (needs/need) sharpening.

　　＜解答＞ need

2687. Scurvy, one of the diseases modern science has conquered, (results/result) from a lack of vitamin C.

　　＜解答＞ results

2688. The British navy, members of which are called " limeys " (was/were) responsible for first using limes to prevent scurvy during long sea voyages.

　　＜解答＞ was

2689. The Boston Pops Orchestra (has/have) greatly increased the enjoyment and appreciation of music for millions of people.

　　＜解答＞　has

2690. The Special Olympics, competitive games for the handicapped, (is/are) an idea
started by the famous Kennedy family.
　　＜解答＞　is

2691. Electronic options, as well as performance, (is/are) important to buyers of new
cars.
　　＜解答＞　are

2692. The Supreme Court's decision, along with discussions of the Justices' opinion,
(is/are) printed in today's newspaper.
　　＜解答＞　is

2693. The beauty of trees in their fall colors (attracts/attract) many tourists to New
England.
　　＜解答＞　attracts

2694. Other animals besides the elephant (is/are) classified as pachyderms.
　　＜解答＞　are

2695. Tsetse flies, which carry the dreadeddisease called sleeping sickness,
(attack/attacks) both humans and cattle.
　　＜解答＞　attack

2696. A single milk pail, in addition to a rothing log and bird tracks, (appears/appear)
in a painting by Andrew Wyeth.
　　＜解答＞　appears

2697. Clean air, as well as clean lakes and rivers, (concerns/concern) all the citizens
of the United States.
　　＜解答＞　concerns

2698. Sufficient amounts of potassium required by the human body (is/are) found in
bananas.
　　＜解答＞　are

2699. Others besides you and me (advocates/advocate) a town cleanup day.
　　＜解答＞　advocate

2700. The effective date of the new regulations for nuclear power plants (have/has) not yet been determined.

＜解答＞ has

2701. The idea that they do not wear out or have to be flipped over (make/makes) compact discs attractive.

＜解答＞ makes

2702. Combustion of oily or gasoline-soaked rags (have/has) been known to occur if they are not stored properly.

＜解答＞ has

2703. Besides having a financial interest in the bay, investors and the local community (use/uses) it for sports and other recreational purposes.

＜解答＞ use

2704. Hot dogs with sauerkraut (is/are) a specialty of the local deli.

＜解答＞ is

2705. Many of the member schools of the state athletic association (refuse/refuses) to abide by the new academic standards.

＜解答＞ refuse

2706. Signs of decay that should be recognized by every citizen (includes/include) oil spills along the shoreline as well as the absence of wildlife.

＜解答＞ include

2707. Not one of the participants in the debate on Central America (was/were) eager to suggest a solution to the problem.

＜解答＞ was

2708. The marketing representative, with the help of her assistant, (is/are) making plans to open a new coffeehouse.

＜解答＞ is

2709. Neither the proposals of the air traffic controllers nor the recommendation of the FAA's committee (have/has) been put into effect.

＜解答＞ has

2710. The debate the rule changes (have/has) apparently thrown the meeting into a deadlock.

　　＜解答＞　has

2711. The public education system for boys and girls in the United States (is/are) intended to stress skills.

　　＜解答＞　is

2712. Alertness, as well as stamina and strength, (is/are) important to rescue workers.

　　＜解答＞　is

2713. Of the world's petroleum, about one third (is/are) produced by the United States.

　　＜解答＞　is

2714. Either brisk walks or jogging (serves/serve) as a healthful way to get daily exercise.

　　＜解答＞　serves

2715. Perhaps the best thing about calculators (is/are) their speed in arriving at accurate answers.

　　＜解答＞　is

2716. On our block alone, ninety-five dollars (were/was) collected for the American Cancer Society.

　　＜解答＞　was

2717. Frutration, failure, and lack of motivation (indicates/indicate) the need to talk with a guidance counselor.

　　＜解答＞　indicate

2718. One sixth of the budget (is/are) allocated to health care.

　　＜解答＞　is

2719. Physics (is/are) taken by the best science students.

　　＜解答＞　is

2720. (Doesn't/Don't) it seem encouraging that the life span of Americans is increasing.

　　＜解答＞　Doesn't

2721. The people with whom I worked last summer (attends/attend) a nearby high school.

　　＜解答＞ attend

2722. The majority of high-school juniors (is/are) familiar with computers.

　　＜解答＞ are

2723. Students who are not finished taking the exam (doesn't/don't) appreciate loud noises in the corridors.

　　＜解答＞ don't

2724. Two teaspoonfuls of cornstarch combined with a small amount of cold water (makes/make) an ideal thickener for many sauces.

　　＜解答＞ makes

2725. The unusual phenomena (was/were) explained by astronomers as being caused by sunspots.

　　＜解答＞ were

2726. It is difficult to make a choice because there (is/are) so many styles of tennis shoes.

　　＜解答＞ are

2727. According to recent government news release, a medical study of world War II veterans (have/has) concluded that the veternans have the same health prospects as nonveterans.

　　＜解答＞ has

2728. Styles in clothing (seem/seems) to change as often as the weather.

　　＜解答＞ seem

2729. The Mexican peso, worth approximately one-half cent, (is/are) easily accepted by the present toll machines.

　　＜解答＞ is

2730. The President, after meeting with several of his advisers, (has/have) promised to veto the proposed tax bill.

　　＜解答＞ has

2731. The list of the best ballplayers of all time (is/are) dominated by outfielders.
  ＜解答＞ is

2732. Some people say that compact discs (offers/offer) a brighter treble and truer bass than conventional records.
  ＜解答＞ offer

2733. The answer that people who like them (gives/give) is that they never wear out because needles never touch them.
  ＜解答＞ give

2734. There (is/are) still other advatages in that compact discs never wear out, and they play over seventy minutes of music on one side.
  ＜解答＞ are

2735. Do you know that compact discs (require/requires) higher quality amplifiers than regular records do ?
  ＜解答＞ require

2736. After a tree has been cut down, the number of rings in the cross section (is/are) significant.
  ＜解答＞ is

2737. Advances in medical research (has/have) nearly eradicated many childhood diseases.
  ＜解答＞ have

2738. When the six o'clock news (comes/come) on, be sure to listen to the weather forecast.
  ＜解答＞ comes

2739. If you see either Veronica or Sabrena in the cafeteria, tell her that I can't meet (them/her) after school today.
  ＜解答＞ her

2740. To learn more about our city government, our civics class (plan/plans) to invite various guest speakers to school.
  ＜解答＞ plans

2741. Over one thousand miles of tunnels (travel/travels) through EI Tienients, the largest copper mine in the world.

　　＜解答＞ travel

2742. The sum of the rings divided by two (tell/tells) you the age of the tree.

　　＜解答＞ tells

2743. Lightening, which is a form of electricity, usually (strikes/strike) the highest or tallest object around.

　　＜解答＞ strikes

2744. For as long as I can remember, the fireworks display (has/have) always started with the arrival of three airborne parachutists.

　　＜解答＞ has

2745. Included on our list (is/are) the mayor, a lawyer, a probation officer, a police officer, and local or state representative.

　　＜解答＞ are

2746. Listening to guest speakers explain and discuss their jobs (makes/make) the class period pass quickly.

　　＜解答＞ makes

2747. I asked my mother whether she would mind (me/my) postponing this chore until later.

　　＜解答＞ my

2748. The author of the story never tells us whether it was (she/her) or her sister who won the contest.

　　＜解答＞ she

2749. One of our teachers, (who/whom) we both like, suggested that we look at the classified advertisements in a newspaper.

　　＜解答＞ whom

2750. We reported our findings to our teacher, (who/whom) we knew would be interested in what we had discovered.

　　＜解答＞ who

2751. A. The ball that was thrown by me was caught by the dog.

   B. The dog caught the ball that I threw.

   ＜解答＞ B

2752. The quilt that (was made by me/I made) won second prize at the county fair.

   ＜解答＞ I made

2753. Frances promised to bring the basket that she (bought/had bought) in Arizona.

   ＜解答＞ had bought

2754. By the time we get to the picnic area, the rain (will stop/will have stopped).

   ＜解答＞ will have stopped

2755. As an eyewitness to the accident, Pam told what (had happened/happened).

   ＜解答＞ had happened

2756. Val claims that cats (make/made) the best pets.

   ＜解答＞ make

2757. The graduation valedictory (will be/will have been) delivered by them.

   ＜解答＞ will have been

2758. I would have lent you my notes if you (had asked/would have asked) me.

   ＜解答＞ had asked

2759. Who has heard that there (are/were) a thousand meters in a kilometer ?

   ＜解答＞ are

2760. The book is on works of art that (have been created/were created) centuries ago.

   ＜解答＞ were created

2761. If I (had listened/would have listened) more carefully, I might have taken better notes.

   ＜解答＞ had listened

2762. The lobbyists (had been/were) waiting an hour before the governor arrived.

   ＜解答＞ had been

2763. We studied Macheth after we (learned/had learned) about the Globe Theatra.

   ＜解答＞ had learned

2764. In August my parents (will have been/will be) married for twenty-five years.
    ＜解答＞ will have been

2765. I would have agreed if you (would have asked/had asked) me sooner.
    ＜解答＞ had asked

2766. My grandmother always said that haste (made/makes) waste.
    ＜解答＞ makes

2767. If the books (were cataloged/have been cataloged) last week, why haven't they been placed on the shelves ?
    ＜解答＞ were cataloged

2768. If he (would have read/had read) " The White Birds, " he might have liked William Butler Yeat's postry.
    ＜解答＞ had read

2769. I'd have tutored you if you (would have asked/had asked) me.
    ＜解答＞ had asked

2770. By next month Ms. Deloney (will be/will have been) mayor for two years.
    ＜解答＞ will have been

2771. Did they know that Labor Day always (came/comes) on the first Monday in September ?
    ＜解答＞ comes

2772. If he (had revised/would have revised) his first draft, he would have received a better grade.
    ＜解答＞ had revised

2773. When you charge the battery in the car, be sure (to have protected/to protect) your eyes and hands from the suffuric acid in the battery.
    ＜解答＞ to protect

2774. Before next Saturday is over, we (will have heard/will hear) some exciting music at the concert.
    ＜解答＞ will have heard

2775. My old skates (lay/have lain) in my closet for the past two years.
    ＜解答＞ have lain

2776. Dave (should have went/should have gone) to the dentist three months ago.

<解答> should have gone

2777. After all of us (had decided/decided) to attend the concert at Boyer Hall, we purchased four tickets for Saturday night.

<解答> had decided

2778. If I (would have known/had known) about the free offer, I would have sent in a coupon.

<解答> had known

2779. I would have liked (to have gone/to go) swimming yesterday.

<解答> to go

2780. If I (had/had had) the address, I would have delivered the package myself.

<解答> had had

2781. After giving me his advice, my math teacher always used to say, " A word to the wise (is/are) sufficient. "

<解答> is

2782. I wish I (read/had read) the chapter before I tried to answer the questions.

<解答> had read

2783. Nathanael West said that (he had/he would) never have written his satirical novels if he had not visited Hollywood.

<解答> he would

2784. Do you think that she would have volunteered to help if she (weren't/wasn't) highly qualified ?

<解答> weren't

2785. In his haste to hand in his test paper, he (would fail/failed) to put his name on it.

<解答> failed

2786. If you (would have remembered/had remembered) to bring something to read, you would not have been so bored.

<解答> had remembered

2787. The smell from the paper mill (laid/lay) over the town like a blanket.

<解答> lay

2788. After the scout had seen the wide receiver in action, he wished he (had offered/offered) the player a scholarship.

<解答> had offered

2789. I wish that I (kept/had kept) in mind that " a stitch in time saves nine. "

<解答> had kept

2790. If Jonathan Edwards (had written/wrote) shorter sentences, we would be even more fascinsted by his messages.

<解答> had written

2791. I'm glad to (have had/have) the opportunity to revise my essay for a higher grade.

<解答> have

2792. If it (was/were) not so cloudy, we would have the party outside.

<解答> were

2793. The rock group (finished/had finished) the concert, but the audience called for another set.

<解答> had finished

2794. If Sherrie had not missed the deadline, the yearbook delivery (had have been/would have been) on time.

<解答> would have been

2795. Although I thought I (had planned/planned) my trip down to the last detail, there was one thing I had forgotten.

<解答> had planned

2796. He would have scored the winning basket if he (would have kept/had kept) his eyes on the clock.

<解答> had kept.

2797. When they returned from picking berries, they (sat/set) their full bowls on the table.

<解答> set

2798. Several books for the research paper (laid/lay) on the desk while he watched TV.

＜解答＞ lay

2799. Any mention of last year's final game (had raised/raised) the coach's ire.

＜解答＞ raised

2800. By the time we (had smelled/smelled) the smoke, the flames had already begun to spread.

＜解答＞ smelled

2801. Even though her standards (were/would be) high, she was considered the most popular teacher in the school.

＜解答＞ were

2802. From our studies we (concluded/had concluded) that woman had played many critical roles in the history of our nation.

＜解答＞ concluded

2803. In 1932, after a flight of almost fifteen hours, Amelia Earhart became the first woman (to have flown/to fly) solo across the Atlantic Ocean.

＜解答＞ to fly

2804. If modern society (was/were) an agricultural one, more of us would know about farming and about the difficulties faced by farmers.

＜解答＞ were

2805. How many of us poses the skills (to have survived/to survive) on our own without the assistance of store-bought items ?

＜解答＞ to have survived

2806. Wacky, my pet chipmunk, was acting as if she (were/was) trying to tell me something.

＜解答＞ were

2807. According to this news article, the concent last Friday night (is/was) " a resounding success. "

＜解答＞ was

2808. Because of the ercessive amount of rain this spring, the water in the dam (has raised/has risen) to a dangerous level.

　　＜解答＞ has risen

2809. By the time you leave high school, you (will have learned/will learn) many interesting facts about history.

　　＜解答＞ will have learned

2810. Factory work is rarely affected by weather conditions, whereas farm work (had always been/has always been) closely interconnected with climate and temperature.

　　＜解答＞ has always been

2811. If you (had taken/would have taken) a nurition class, you would have learned how to shop wisely for food.

　　＜解答＞ had taken

2812. A. Yesterday, Dad's car was washed and waxed by my brother.

　　B. Yesterday, my brother washed and waxed Dad's car.

　　＜解答＞ B

2813. A. At the retirement party, the principal gave our teacher a gift.

　　B. At the retirement party, our teacher was given a gift by the principal.

　　＜解答＞ A

2814. After spending the entire morning working in the garden, Jim (is laying/is lying) down for a rest.

　　＜解答＞ is lying

2815. This car is roomier than (any/any other) car we ever had.

　　＜解答＞ any other

2816. My geometry grades were higher than (anyone's/anyone else's) in my class.

　　＜解答＞ anyone else's

2817. Which do you think is (worse/worser), finding a worm in your apple or finding half a worm ?

　　＜解答＞ worse

2818. You have to look very (careful/carefully) to see the watermark on this postage stamp.

　　　＜解答＞　carefully

2819. I felt (awfully/awful) after eating all that food.

　　　＜解答＞　awful

2820. I tried to explain why I was late, but my mother looked at me (skeptical/skeptically).

　　　＜解答＞　skeptically

2821. When Mrs. Hayes calls on me in chemistry class, I can't help (but feel/feeling) nervous and uncertain.

　　　＜解答＞　feeling

2822. As I waited anxiously in the airport, I still (had no/didn't have no) way of knowing if Laura May had managed to catch the flight.

　　　＜解答＞　had no

2823. (Since/Being that) I did nothing to antagonize that Doberman, I can't understand why it bit me.

　　　＜解答＞　Since

2824. If you want to find additional information about Southtown, you (had ought/ought) to go to the library.

　　　＜解答＞　ought

2825. The (Gallaghers/Gallaghers they) have worked for years to increase voter registration in this town.

　　　＜解答＞　Gallaghers

2826. (Being that/Because) Jennifer has never learned to swin, she is afraid to go on the boat ride.

　　　＜解答＞　Because

2827. (Can't none/Can't any) of the people in town see that the mayor is appointing political cronies to patronage jobs ?

　　　＜解答＞　Can't any

2828. What (kind of/kind of a) person would assassinate the President of the United States ?

＜解答＞ kind of

2829. Sometimes I get so absorbed in a movie that I forget where I (am/am at).

＜解答＞ am

2830. After looking everywhere for my tip clip, I gave up. But I didn't care about it that much (anyways/anyway).

＜解答＞ anyway

2831. The swings in the park are rusting (some/somewhat).

＜解答＞ somewhat

2832. Since I didn't have (no/any) homework, I dicided to go out to shoot some baskets.

＜解答＞ any

2833. The reason the book was so difficult to understand was (because/that) the writing was unclear.

＜解答＞ that

2834. The discovery and development of synthetic fibers required an (ingenious/ingenuous) mind.

＜解答＞ ingenious

2835. Automation in the coal fields has put thousands of (miners/minors) out of work.

＜解答＞ miners

2836. Denise makes a big point of (flouting/flounting) the lunchroom rules.

＜解答＞ flouting

2837. The old man looked at his first Christmas tree in (childish/childlike) wonder.

＜解答＞ childike

2838. The Puritans believed that God was (immanent/imminent) in all of the natural world.

＜解答＞ immanent

2839. Nora told yet another (anecdote/antidote) about her trip to Pikes Peak.

　　　＜解答＞　anecdote

2840. The spy received (oral/verbal) directions, rather than written ones.

　　　＜解答＞　oral

2841. Cicero's name was on the (prescribed/proscribed) list, which meant he was a criminal who could be killed by anyone.

　　　＜解答＞　proscribed

2842. Ellsworth will (prosecute/persecute) his case against the fast-food chain.

　　　＜解答＞　prosecute

2843. Which European leaders (capitalized/capitulated) to the Nazis ?

　　　＜解答＞　capitulated

2844. Its large size, simple structure, and (how readily available it is/ready availability) make the common cockroach convenient to study.

　　　＜解答＞　ready availability

2845. They are (found not only/not only found) in urban areas but in the tropics.

　　　＜解答＞　found not only

2846. Cockroach eggs are laid in small cases, carried on the female body, and then (deposited/they deposit them) in hidden crevices.

　　　＜解答＞　deposited

2847. Cockroachs will eat anything, but they especially like sweet foods and(foods that are starchy/starchy foods).

　　　＜解答＞　starchy foods

2848. The cockroach (is both/both is) the most primitive living winged insect and the most ancient fossil insect.

　　　＜解答＞　is both

2849. Cockroackes have smooth, leathery skin; long, thin antennae; and (they have a body that is thick and flat/a thick, flat body).

　　　＜解答＞　a thick, flat body

2850. Cockroaches may be dark brown, pale brown, or (delicate green/of a green color that is delicate).

　　　　　＜解答＞　delicate green

2851. A typical cockroach lives as a nymph for about a year, and as an adult (for about half a year/its life lasts about half a year).

　　　　　＜解答＞　for about half a year

2852. A. We might not only view the cockroach with disgust but also interest.

　　　　B. We might view the cockroach not only with disgust but also with interest.

　　　　　＜解答＞　B

2853. We have as much to learn from the cochroach's evolution as (we have to gain from its extinction/there is to gain from extinguishing it).

　　　　　＜解答＞　we have to gain from its extinction

2854. Mr. Connor's lecture are easier to comprehend than (Ms. Moore/those of Ms. Moore).

　　　　　＜解答＞　those of Ms. Moore

2855. A dog's ability to hear-pitched sounds is much keener than (that of humans/humans).

　　　　　＜解答＞　that of humans

2856. The biographical information in the encyclopedia is more detailed than (the dictionary/that in the dictionary).

　　　　　＜解答＞　that in the dictionary

2857. The view from the World Trade Center is even more spectacular than the (one from the Empire State Building/Empire State Building).

　　　　　＜解答＞　one from the Empire State Building

2858. Some birds like to eat fruits as much as (insects/insects do).

　　　　　＜解答＞　insects do

2859. A modern director's interpretation of Hamlet is very different from (a nineteenth-century director/a nineteenth-century director's).

　　　　　＜解答＞　a nineteenth-century director's

2860. How do your grades in English compare with (science/your grades in science).

　　　　　＜解答＞　your grades in science

2861. People have been more interested in reading the book than (in seeing the movie version/the movie version).

<解答> in seeing the movie version

2862. The strength in my left hand is greater than (that in my right hand/my right hand).

<解答> that in my right hand

2863. This month the price of gold has risen more sharply than (that of silver/silver).

<解答> that of silver

2864. One of the accident victims suffered a broken arm, several broken ribs, and (one of her lungs was punctured/a punctured lung).

<解答> a punctured lung

2865. As we left the harbor, the radio weather report predicted gale-force winds, heavy rain, and (abnormally high tides/that tides would be abnormally high).

<解答> abnormally high tides

2866. She spoke about her experience in Australia and (A. made several predictions about the country's future/B. several predictions about the country's future).

<解答> A

2867. The unexpected cooperation of China was a greater surprise to Russia than (the Untied States/to the United States).

<解答> to the United States

2868. We were not sure that our request for a raise was fair or (it would be granted/that it would be granted).

<解答> that it would be granted

2869. Attention has been centered on the need for more teachers, adequate classroom, and (enough new equipment/there isn't enough new equipment).

<解答> enough new equipment

2870. The ambassador did not know whether the President (A. had sent for him or the Secretary of State/B. or the Secretayr of State had sent for him).

<解答> B

2871. The players were annoyed not so much by the decisions of the officials as (by the hostile/the hostile) crowd.

    ＜解答＞ by the hostile

2872. The headmaster insisted that all of us return by ten o'clock and (that the housemasters check us in/the housemasters must check us in).

    ＜解答＞ that the housemasters check us in

2873. Pioneers came with hopes of being happy and free and (to made/of making) their fortunes in the new world.

    ＜解答＞ of making

2874. A. She not only was industrious, but she could be depended on.

    B. She was not only industrious but also dependable.

    ＜解答＞ B

2875. A cloudy day is better for a game than (a sunny day/sunshine).

    ＜解答＞ a sunny day

2876. To the anthinking person, war may be a romantic adventure, (A. but a foolish and dirty business is the way the wise person regards it/B. but to the wise person it is a foolish and dirty business).

    ＜解答＞ B

2877. The skipper had a harsh voice, a weatherbeaten face, and (a very stocky build/was very stocky in build).

    ＜解答＞ a very stocky build

2878. The speech of cultivated Britishers is not so different as it used to be from (the speech of cultivated Americans/Americans).

    ＜解答＞ the speech of cultivated Americans

2879. This was a much harder assignment for me than (for Luis/Luis).

    ＜解答＞for Luis

2880. A. Her friends were not only shocked but also greatly disappointed by her failure./B. Her friends not only were shocked by her failure but they felt a great disappointment.

    ＜解答＞ A

2881. The company announced a bonus for all five-year employees and (A. that deserving new employees would be give additional benefits/B. additional benefits for deserving new employees).

＜解答＞　B

2882. High-school programs have been accused of being too closely tied in with college education and (of neglecting/that they neglect) the average teen-ager.

＜解答＞　of neglecting

2883. All delegates to the convention were advised that on their return they would (both have to make/have to make both) a written and oral report.

＜解答＞　have to make both

2884. A. band with two trupet players and thirty-five clarinetists (sound/sounds) terrible.

＜解答＞　sounds

2885. The chemicals that sometimes leak out of a sewer system or waste dump (contaminates/contaminate) aquifers.

＜解答＞　contaminate

2886. When the math team came in second, the team members were upset because they (hoped/ had hoped) to take first place.

＜解答＞　had hoped

2887. The tree died because it (was hit/had been hit) by lightning.

＜解答＞　had been hit

2888. The five riders are pleased (to qualify/to have qualified) for the equestrian team.

＜解答＞　to have qualified

2889. Pam finally appreciated the old saying that every cloud (had/has) a silver lining.

＜解答＞　has

2890. Although Denny's skill (had been demonstrated/was demonstrated) during the season, he was not selected to play in the city All-Star game.

＜解答＞　had been demonstrated

2891. When I finally got to the dentist, my tooth already (stopped/had stopped) hurting.

　　＜解答＞　had stopped

2892. When I presented my speech before the committee, the members previously (studied/had studied) several reports on nuclear waste disposal.

　　＜解答＞　had studied

2893. By then I (will have received/will receive) my first paycheck.

　　＜解答＞　will have received

2894. The judges declared that we (made/ had made) the most interesting exhibit at the science fair.

　　＜解答＞　had made

2895. As I thought about our argument, I was sure you (had lost/lost) your temper first.

　　＜解答＞　had lost

2896. When we viewed the videotapes of the game, we saw that the other team (committed/had committed) the foul.

　　＜解答＞　had committed

2897. How could I have forgotten that Great Britain (included/includes) England, Wales, and Scotland ?

　　＜解答＞　includes

2898. If Gary (had read/would have read) the advertisement, he could have saved a hundred dollars on that camera.

　　＜解答＞　had read

2899. By the time we graduate in June, Ms. O'connell (will be/will have been) teaching Latin for twenty-four years.

　　＜解答＞　will have been

2900. If they (had/had had) enoug money, they could have taken a taxi.

　　＜解答＞　had had

2901. (Spending/Having spent) three hours on a review of chemistry, we then worked on irregular French verbs.

<解答>　Having spent

2902. A. I should have liked to have met them./B. I should have liked to meet them.

<解答>　B

2903. Sometimes before the bus leaves, I (will finish/will have finished) packing.

<解答>　will have finished

2904. We were hoping (to have/to have had) a short-answer test in history instead of an essay exam.

<解答>　to have

2905. Gloria was confused all day because it seemed as though it (was/were) Friday, but it was only Thursday.

<解答>　were

2906. In preparing for a job interview, you should wear styles and colors of clothing that look (attractive/ attractively) on you.

<解答>　attractive

2907. Lionel gave a (credible/credulous) account of how he had spent so much money on his vacation.

<解答>　credible

2908. Whenever I'm not doing (something/nothing) challenging, I grow bored easily.

<解答>　something

2909. We were grateful to our knowledgealbe (coach, who guided/coach and who guided) us patiently throughout the year.

<解答>　coach, who guided

2910. Blacklighting (A. is when the main source of light is placed behind/B. is the placement of the main source of light behind) the subject being photographed.

<解答>　B

2911. He has been the catcher for every game this year, and he is beginning to look (kind of tired/rather tired).

<解答>　rather tired

2912. As soon as we returned to the campsite, we discovered that someone (took/had taken) our food and gear.

<解答> had taken

2913. The racing car went out of control (before/before it) hit the barrier.

<解答> before it

2914. When (she got/got) on the train, Mrs. Tomkins realized she had made a dreadful mistake.

<解答> she got

2915. The racing car went out of control (and hit/hit) the barrier several times before it came to a stop on a grassy bank.

<解答> and hit

2916. (That money/Money) doesn't grow on tress should be obvious.

<解答> That money

2917. The dealer told me how much he was prepared to pay for my car and (that I/I) could have the money without delay.

<解答> that I

2918. He (boasted about/boasted) how successful he was.

<解答> boasted about

2919. (Whether/Of) he has signed the contract doesn't matter.

<解答> Whether

2920. I'm concerned about (whether/if) he has signed the contract.

<解答> whether

2921. He is the man (who he/who) lives next door.

<解答> who

2922. The cat (which it/which) caught the mouse.

<解答> which

2923. The Thames, (that/which) is now clear enough to swim in, was polluted for over a hundred years.

<解答> which

2924. He is the man that I (met him/met) on holiday.

<解答> met

2925. He is the man (to whom/who) I gave the money.

　　＜解答＞　to whom

2926. Everything (that/which) can be done has been done.

　　＜解答＞　that

2927. (Since/Because) I phoned you this morning, I have changed my plans.

　　＜解答＞　Since

2928. A. Reading my newspaper, I heard the doorbell ring.

　　B. Reading my newspaper, the doorbell rang.

　　＜解答＞　A

2929. A. Seated in the presidential car, the crowd wave to the Prsident.

　　B. Seated in the presidential car, the President waved to the crowd.

　　＜解答＞　B

2930. A. We preferred the house painted white.

　　B. Painted white, we preferred the house.

　　＜解答＞　A

2931. All means (have/has) been used to get him to change his mind.

　　＜解答＞　have

2932. One means (is/are) still to be tried.

　　＜解答＞　is

2933. A pair of glasses (cost/costs) quite a lot these days.

　　＜解答＞　costs

2934. Two pairs of your trousers (are/is) still at the cleaner's.

　　＜解答＞　are

2935. Three weeks (are/is) a long time to wait for an answer.

　　＜解答＞　is

2936. Two hundred pounds (is/are) a lot to spend on a dress.

　　＜解答＞　is

2937. Forty miles (is/are) a long way to walk in a day.

　　＜解答＞　is

2938. You cannot omit (an/a) H in that word.

    ＜解答＞ an

2939. A. My friend invited me to dinner./B. My friend, he invited me to dinner.

    ＜解答＞ A

2940. A. My car, I parked it outside./B. I parked my car outside.

    ＜解答＞ B

2941. What do you think of this cake ? I (like it/like).

    ＜解答＞ like it

2942. What do you think of these cakes ? I don't (like/like them).

    ＜解答＞ like them

2943. A. He punched me in the face./B. He punched my face.

    ＜解答＞ A

2944. The soldier (absented/absented himself) without leave for three weeks.

    ＜解答＞ absented himself

2945. I haven't got any money on (me/myself).

    ＜解答＞ me

2946. (Not/No) much is happening in our office at the moment.

    ＜解答＞ Not

2947. She's had (not/no) a few proposals of marriage in her time.

    ＜解答＞ not

2948. He's angry because my marks are the same (as/like) his.

    ＜解答＞ as

2949. (Go and buy/Go to buy) yourself a new pair of shoes.

    ＜解答＞ Go and buy

2950. He (had/had got) long hair when he was a teenager.

    ＜解答＞ had

2951. (I have/I'd) a cold shower every morning.

    ＜解答＞ I have

2952. Could they rescue the cat on the roof ? A few people said: " No, they couldn't.
    " But some people said: " Yes, they (could/managed to). "

<解答>　managed to

2953. I (couldn't/didn't) imagine what it would be like to live in a hot.

<解答>　couldn't

2954. May I borrow your umbrella please ? No, you (may not/might not).

<解答>　may not

2955. You (can/could) watch TV for as long as you like.

<解答>　can

2956. He used to live in Los Angles and so (used/did) I.

<解答>　did

2957. I never used to eat a large breakfast, but I (eat/do) now.

<解答>　do

2958. I (lived/used to live) in the country for three years.

<解答>　lived

2959. If he (should/will) call, tell him I'll ring back.

<解答>　should

2960. If you (shouldn't/don't) stay up so late every evening, you won't feel so sleepy in the morning.

<解答>　don't

2961. I (won't/wouldn't) be surprised if he didn't try to blackmail you.

<解答>　wouldn't

2962. If you (don't/didn't) stay up so late every evening, you wouldn't feel so sleepy in the morning.

<解答>　didn't

2963. If I (were/was) in your position, I'd accept their offer.

<解答>　were

2964. If I were Jame, I (had/would) walk out on him.

<解答>　would

2965. If it (weren't/wasn't) for your help, I would still be homeless.

<解答>　weren't

2966. (Were it not/Weren't it) for your help, I would still be homeless.

<解答> Were it not

2967. If he (were/is) to ask, would you help him ?

<解答> were

2968. If Sue were to make an effort, she (can/could) do better.

<解答> could

2969. (Were/Was) the government to cut Value Added Tax, prices would fall.

<解答> Were

2970. If it (has/had) been raining this morning, we would have stayed at home.

<解答> had

2971. If I had not got married, I (would/will) still have been living abroad.

<解答> would

2972. If I (had/have) been in your position, I'd have accepted their offer.

<解答> had

2973. If it hadn't been for the rain, we (would/had) have had a good harvest.

<解答> would

2974. (Had/Should) the management acted sooner, the strike wouldn't have happened.

<解答> Had

2975. (Had it not/Hadn't it) been for the unusually bad weather, the rescue party would have been able to save the stranded climber.

<解答> Had it not

2976. You'll have to put up with it, (whether/if) you like it or not.

<解答> whether

2977. " Are you all right ? " he (said/told me).

<解答> said

2978. " You haven't got much time, he (told/said) me.

<解答> told

2979. He told me he (has/had) to warn me of the consequences.

<解答> had

2980. He wants to know (whether or not/if or not) we want dinner.

　　＜解答＞　whether or not

2981. How can I help my children not (worry/to worry) about their exams ?

　　＜解答＞　to worry

2982. He was known (to have/have) a quick temper as a boy.

　　＜解答＞　to have

2983. I'd like to lie down and (go/to go) to sleep.

　　＜解答＞　go

2984. A. I think it best to go./B. I think to go is best.

　　＜解答＞　A

2985. We soon (learnt/how) to do as we were told in Mr. Lee's class !

　　＜解答＞　learnt

2986. I have a meal (to prepare/to be prepared).

　　＜解答＞　to prepare

2987. (Sue/It) is frantic getting everything ready for the wedding.

　　＜解答＞　Sue

2988. I dread (to think/thinking) what has happened to him.

　　＜解答＞　to think

2989. I dread (going/to go) to the dentist.

　　＜解答＞　going

2990. He's been gardening (all day/for all day).

　　＜解答＞　all day

2991. Since 1971, Britain (has/has had) decimal currency.

　　＜解答＞　has had

2992. I am feeling (very/much) more healthy than I was.

　　＜解答＞　much

2993. I'd prefer a large bottle to a (small/small one).

　　＜解答＞　small one

2994. A. It was by train that we reached New York.

　　B. How we reached New York was by train.

<解答> A

2995. A. Who met us was the ambassador./B. It was the ambassador that met us.
    <解答> B

2996. A. What he is a genius./B. It's a genius that he is.
    <解答> A

2997. A. What he's done is spoil the whole thing.
    B. It's spoil the whole thing that he's done.
    <解答> A

2998. A. That she slipped arsenic in his tea is said.
    B. It is said that she slipped arsenic in his tea.
    <解答> B

2999. A. I'll leave it to you to lock the door./B. I'll leave to lock the door to you.
    <解答> A

3000. A. More people than used to years ago own house these days.
    B. More people own houses these days than used to years ago.
    <解答> B

3001. A. He showed less pity than any other tyrant in history to his victims.
    B. He showed less pity to his victims than any other tyrant in history to his victims.
    <解答> B

3002. A. He gave away them./B. He gave them away.
    <解答> B

3003. A. The people involved were reported to the police.
    B. The involved people were reported to the police.
    <解答> A

3004. A. The men present were his supporters.
    B. The present men were his supporters.
    <解答> A

3005. A. These are too heavy boxes to carry./B. These boxes are too heavy to carry.
    <解答> B

3006. A. The box is so heavy that I can't carry it.

B. This is a heavy box that I can't carry it.

＜解答＞ A

3007. A. He put the point well./B. He well put the point.

＜解答＞ A

3008. A. In Chinese restaurants many people eat in London.

B. In London many people eat in Chinese restaurants.

＜解答＞ B

3009. (How/What) strange a feeling it was !

＜解答＞ How

3010. (What/How) starnge ideas you have !

＜解答＞ What

3011. The Prime Minister (is/will be) to make a statement tomorrow.

＜解答＞ is

3012. A great number of guests (were/was) there.

＜解答＞ were

3013. There (was/were) lots of food on the table.

＜解答＞ was

3014. (Having/Have) left before the letter arrived, he was surprised to find his wife at the station.

＜解答＞ Having

3015. We were (allowed/wanted) to stay another week.

＜解答＞ allowed

3016. What (caused/got) them to revise their decision ?

＜解答＞ caused

3017. (The farther/Farther) north you go, the more severe the winters are.

＜解答＞ The farther

3018. The more you argue with him, (the less/less) notice he takes.

＜解答＞ the less

3019. We'll have to begin our journey early tomorrow; in fact, the (early/earlier), the better.

<解答> earlier

3020. John plays tennis, and (so does/does) his sister.

<解答> so does

國家圖書館出版品預行編目資料

TOEFL 托福文法與構句／李英松著. ─初版.─
新北市：李昭儀，2022.10
　　冊；　公分
ISBN 978-957-43-9951-2（中冊 : 平裝）
ISBN 978-957-43-9952-9（下冊 : 平裝）
1.CST: 托福考試 2.CST: 語法
805.1894　　　　　　　　111004270

TOEFL托福文法與構句 下冊

作　　者　李英松

發 行 人　李英松

出　　版　李昭儀
　　　　　Email：lambtyger@gmail.com

設計編印　白象文化事業有限公司
　　　　　專案主編：李婕　　經紀人：徐錦淳

經銷代理　白象文化事業有限公司
　　　　　412台中市大里區科技路1號8樓之2（台中軟體園區）
　　　　　出版專線：（04）2496-5995　　傳真：（04）2496-9901
　　　　　401台中市東區和平街228巷44號（經銷部）
　　　　　購書專線：（04）2220-8589　　傳真：（04）2220-8505

印　　刷　普羅文化股份有限公司

初版一刷　2022 年 10 月

定　　價　420 元

白象文化
www.ElephantWhite.com.tw

印書小舖
PressStore 出版雜記

出 版・經 銷・宣 傳・設 計

f 自費出版的領導者

購書 白象文化生活館